the Buffalo Tree

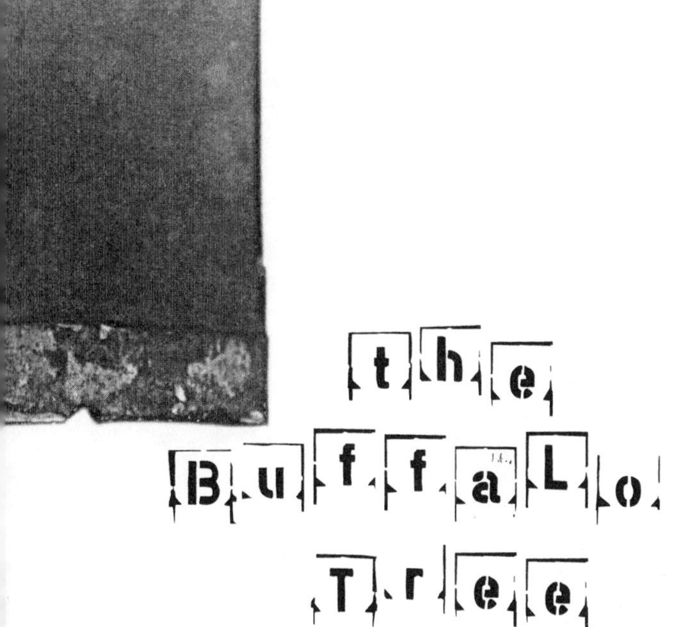

adam rapp

FRONT STREET
Asheville, North Carolina

Thank you, Walt,
and thank you, Stephen

Printed in the United States of America
First Front Street paperback edition, 2007

The Library of Congress has cataloged the hardcover edition of this book as follows:

Library of Congress Cataloging-in-Publication Data
Rapp, Adam.
The buffalo tree / Adam Rapp. — 1st ed.
p. cm.
Summary: While serving a six-month sentence at a juvenile detention center, thirteen-year-old Sura struggles to survive the experience with his spirit intact.
ISBN 1-886910-19-7 (alk. paper)
[1. Juvenile detention homes—Fiction. 2. Self-reliance—Fiction.] I. Title.
PZ7.R18133Bu 1997 [Fic]—dc21 96-54698
Paperback ISBN 978-1-932425-99-4

Front Street
An Imprint of Boyds Mills Press, Inc.
A Highlights Company
815 Church Street
Honesdale, Pennsylvania 18431

for

Mary Lee Rapp

WE ARE PLAYING FLOOR HOCKEY IN THE basement of Spalding Cottage. The light cage keeps getting hit and that bulb is about to bust. When it swings you can see those long shadows creeping on the wall.

There are fifteen juvies and most of us ain't sporting shirts. When a bunch of juvies get to playing some floor hockey in the basement of Spalding you get that thick, cooked smell.

Some juvies are playing just to feel their bodies fighting, to throw some bows and bust you in the ribs, and some are mad slashing for that puck. I am playing cause Coly Jo is playing, and I like the sound of those sticks hitting each other. I am playing cause my hands are faster than theirs.

I am the only white juvy. I got a thought that if I was outside of my body and watching from the ceiling, I would look like deadness in the mass of their shiny, boiling dark, like some puppet bones.

I get my stick on the puck and flick it. I am smaller than them but I am quicker and I know they can smell the quickness on me, the same way you know about quickness when a rat is in a kitchen. They can smell it on my back when I get low and use my legs.

I am the fastest juvy in Spalding. Sometimes another juvy wants to race me. He gets those happy feet up and waits for me outside the hash house. And juvies bunch up on the other side of the parking lot and put three or four tenths on the race. Then someone whistles through his fingers and I'm off with the quickness and that wind gets up in my ears and—*Go, Sura!*—eleven or twelve seconds later I got me another rabbit. That's what I call those juvies who want to race me and wait for me outside the hash house like that—rabbits. Sometimes I'll even let that juvy get a head start on me so I get a challenge.

Today I dusted Jona Kimbrough and he was sporting some track shoes.

Coly Jo plays floor hockey in his jeans cause that's all he's got. His unbreakable comb keeps falling out of his pocket and he keeps picking it up. He's always trying to bust those naps with that comb. Sometimes he'll just stick it in his Afro and walk around.

Coly Jo is my patch mate. When someone throws me into the wall Coly Jo goes after him and gets that juvy with his stick.

Coly Jo and I have been here six weeks and after blackout we take turns sleeping cause Hodge or Boo Boxfoot will creep into your room and crib shit. Hodge and Boo are on their third clip. A clip is like a year but it ain't the same. Most juvy homes don't give clips. They let you go when you make reform. But Hamstock is different. It's like Hamstock wants to keep you.

Boo and Hodge know the halls and the shadows and the tricks in the showers. I've seen how Hodge sweet-talks those old hash house Honeys into extra slices of pie. I've seen the Mop Man slip a fifth of Old Crow into Boo's laundry bundle.

They cribbed most of Coly Jo's shit his first two days. I heard them in our room after blackout, creeping like some cats. Boo sports Coly Jo's Barnum Fletcher squirrel-skin cap around Spalding like it's something his moms sent him. He's sporting it right now and the tail keeps flipping up.

Boo's got a harelip and he makes me rent a bedside table for six tenths a week. That's half your juvy pound. And you get that only if you don't get carped. They'll carp you with the quickness for walking into Spalding with your shoes on and cut away two tenths. And you'll be in line for your weekly juvy pound and they'll just take out their little notebook and cross off some digits and hand you four or six tenths instead of that full bone-and-twenty. And they don't even look at you either; they just shove that change at you like it's some medicine you got to take.

And they'll carp you if you don't call them Mister, too. If you get carped enough they'll send you to Dean Petty and they say he's got a two-foot paddle with air holes. I ain't seen it yet, but they talk about it the way you talk about boogymonsters and sharks. They say it was made from some body-box wood and that he hangs it over his desk. But if you're smart you won't get carped.

That table Boo makes me rent wobbles and creaks, but it can hold pens and shit.

At the hash house Coly Jo tells the other juvies how he's going to get his cap back, how he's going to put a whipping on Hodge and Boo. Most of them laugh, though, cause Coly Jo is fat and he don't sport a belt right and sometimes his ass will creep up out of his drawers like some dark blobfish.

But I've seen Coly Jo stare at them. He does it privately and from a distance. His eyes go yellow like a sick dog's.

On my third day they cribbed my electronic football game. Sometimes I can hear them playing it after blackout. I can hear their voices and I can hear my game beating them and I can hear their hands moving in secret. But their hands ain't faster than mines.

There ain't no windows in the basement and those hair vapors keep getting in my mouth. I tried to comb some of Coly Jo's wave grease into my hair last week, but all it did was make my hair look vinyl. Wave grease's got that medicine smell that the Honeys like. I know this cause before I got caught clipping hoodies I used to watch the Honeys from Choate Street sneaking whiffs of wave grease in the pharmacy where I would crib my squares. Newports got that smooth toothpaste smell and they usually set them right up on the counter. I never smoke them, though, cause it ain't good for your lungwind.

You got to keep your lungwind up to clip hoodies; you never know when you might get chased. One night I got chased by a man with a fake arm. I clipped his '77 Lincoln Clown Car and he chased me clear across town and his arm was mad flying off his side like a machine with little spoked parts. I finally lost him after I slipped into a church and cut through the evening service. I ran right over the altar and out the back. I took a week off after that.

A Lincoln hoody might go for two bones and that's only if it shines right.

So you can't smoke squares if you're clipping hoodies. But I'll stick a square on my ear when I go roller skating. I'll put a piece of tape on it so it stays, too. And I'll throw on a pair of wristbands and sport my Red Troutman's fireproof windbreaker and the Honeys will grab at the Newport on my ear and call me *Sura, Sura* and laugh and get mad sexy. I'm mad sexy myself—especially when I double up on the wristbands and fold my windbreaker over a chair so the wrinkles fall smooth.

You got to be fast to clip hoodies. And you need a good pair of wire cutters and that buttonlock grip. Slider taught me how to do the buttonlock last spring. You roll those fingers tight into your thumb and pull that hoody back so the cord goes tight. If your buttonlock is strong enough that hoody will pop off like the head of a dandyweed.

Slider was here for a while, but he got sent down to St. Charles when he turned sixteen. Slider tried to set his pops's house on fire. Around here they call St. Charles "St. Chuck's."

The puck is everywhere and I don't know whose side I'm on no more. The game has lost its game sense. I just keep looking for Coly Jo. The score don't matter. As long as you keep moving and hit with your arms and stay quick to not get hit, then you can feel like you've won.

Suddenly the puck spits out from the scramble like a big medicine pill. It spins on its side for a moment and drops dead. I wonder why no one is fighting for it.

The shouts grow louder and someone's knocked the light again and it's throwing shadows off of those dark juvy faces. I see Boo rise up with his stick and hack down. That squirrel-skin cap ain't on his head no more and you can see the small dents in his clean skull. I rush toward those busting arms and I can see Hodge in the middle. He's got Coly Jo pinned down. Coly Jo is holding his squirrel-skin cap like you hold on to that lucky rabbit's foot when you're slinging some craps. Someone is trying to crib it out of his hand. Boo just hacks down with that stick.

Some juvies are cheering and others have backed away into their own private knots. Coly Jo's shirt's been ripped off and his skin is dark and shiny like a new street and there are marks on his soft belly that look like red crow feet.

I am lunging for Boo when I am pulled back and thrown into the wall again. I am on the ground now and juvies are shouting and scraping sticks on the concrete floor and no one cares about that orange puck.

Under the shouts I can hear Coly Jo's voice. It's more like a non-voice. I can hear him trying to not-cry. I can hear how that scream is stuck in his stomach. I try to get up again but someone beats me on my back and I can't see cause hands are mad pressed over my face. When some hands are pressed on your face like that you can smell the blood in them and you can feel how hot they are.

Somewhere there is a slamming door and a loud whistle that sounds like a Honey shrieking and then those hands disappear and there is a quick silence like you hear in the street after some cars crash.

Mister Rose stands at the entrance of the basement. Mister Rose is our cottage pops. He lives on the first floor of Spalding and he's got a color TV that you can hear sometimes if you stand in that sweet spot in the basement. It's pretty smooth if he's got those skin flicks on.

Mister Rose eats a lot of barbecue potato chips and his fingers are always orange. The juice in his hair makes it look electric. The whistle falls from his face and he yells, "Lock up!" and everyone drops their sticks and locks up. When you lock up you stand up straight and lock those knees and tuck your chin into your chest.

You can see Coly Jo's belly hanging over his jeans. It's all cut up and swollen. Coly Jo is fat and he is afraid of the dark and sometimes in the patch he'll cry into the back of his elbow when you ain't looking.

Boo is sporting the squirrel-skin cap again.

Mister Rose stands there for a long time. He'll sometimes stare at you like that and you start to feel like someone's messed with the thermostat. All you can hear are juvies smoothing out their lungwind.

Mister Rose twirls the whistle leash around his orange fingers. His face starts to mad sweat and he wipes it smooth with a rag. He watches us with those far-spread eyes. Sometimes he looks like a cooked shark.

"You juvies only had one more click," he says.

A click is the sound that the night guard makes with his ribstick every time he passes the iron hitchpost in front of Spalding. It's called a ribstick cause he'll bust you in the side if he catches you running for the fence. You usually get three clicks' worth of free time before blackout.

"One more click," Mister Rose says again. "You juvies was doin just fine." Mister Rose bends down and picks up the puck and looks at it and then cleans it with his thumb.

"Shep, what transpired?" he asks, his arms folded at his chest now. Mister Rose will use a dictionary word like "transpired" every now and then. He reads those word books when he's watching us at study box.

"They was chuckin, Mister Rose," Shep says.

"Who was chuckin?"

Shep don't answer. I can hear something jump in his throat.

"Who was chuckin, Shep?" Mister Rose asks again, his voice still soft.

"I couldn't tell, Mister Rose."

"You couldn't tell."

"I thought it was the game, Mister Rose."

"The game."

"I thought they was goin for the puck, Mister Rose."

"Who?" Mister Rose asks.

Shep pauses a moment and then goes, "Coly Jo, Mister Rose."

"And who else?"

"I couldn't see, Mister Rose."

Mister Rose points to Coly Jo and calls him over with his finger. Coly Jo steps out of line and walks over.

"Who was you chuckin with, Coly Jo?" Mister Rose asks, bending down to tie his shoes. He sports those burnt-looking Dr. J's that are all worn out on the floors. And he sports them with those dirty laces, too, like he's had them for about fifty clips. Sometimes they squeak if he steps wrong.

Coly Jo just shakes his head.

"You don't know who you was chuckin with?" Mister Rose asks.

"I was just chuckin cause they was chuckin, Mister Rose," he replies. I want Coly Jo to tell Mister Rose about his cap and how Boo cribbed it, but I know he won't. His hand hangs over his red belly. It don't look right when a black kid bleeds. The blood looks like something you put on a cake.

Mister Rose keeps staring at him. The only sound is Coly Jo's nose holes mad sucking that hot air.

"Pick someone, then," Mister Rose says.

Coly Jo looks up at Mister Rose.

"Go on and pick out one of these juvies so we can finish chuckin and get to blackout. Can't go to blackout on no half-chuck."

Coly Jo stands there, his hand draped over his stomach.

"Go on," Mister Rose says.

Coly Jo won't look at us. He just looks down at the floor. That juvy quiet's gotten thicker.

Coly Jo looks up and his face is wet and the whites of his eyes go wide and his hand is moving the way fire moves. He can't stop it.

I step forward.

"Sura?" Mister Rose says.

"I'll chuck with him, Mister Rose," I say.

"Your patch mate?" Mister Rose says.

"Yes sir, Mister Rose."

Mister Rose looks at me and then at Coly Jo. I think he might laugh or adjust his false teeth, but he just stands there with that non-look on his face.

"So long as we get some sleep," he says, and directs the rest of the juvies to circle around us.

I know we got to hit for real and I know I will be hurt cause Coly Jo is bigger than me. But he is fat and slow and afraid of the dark and his belly's already been softened. I just got to be fast and take his punches.

"Chuck until the click, now," Mister Rose says.

Coly Jo talks to me with his eyes, and I try to talk back to him with mines. Mines say *Easy, man. Easy.*

Then Mister Rose busts us on our backs and the shouts rise up like some wind blowing through old trees and Coly Jo and I are chucking with the quickness.

We are on the floor and he's wrapped his arms around my head and he is mad whispering into my ear.

"Go on and hit me," he is saying. "Go on, Sura."

And then his arms go slack and I wheel around and stick him in his eye. And then he sticks me in my mouth. We are making a good chuck. We are pressing hard against each other and I am using my legs. His eye is closing up and my lip is split. I can hear some of those juvy voices calling out my name and I wonder why those juvy voices will only call your name out like that when you're chucking.

Coly Jo has climbed onto my back and I can feel his fists on the back of my head, but they are soft and I hope he is making the right kind of face so that Mister Rose will believe those fists. I slide under Coly Jo and charge at his cut belly and he falls back and I stick him in his ear.

My lungwind is mad cooking and I think I'm going to bust some throw-up but I swallow hard and I look up at Coly Jo and he looks like he is going to bust some throw-up, too, and then you can't hear nothing for a second and then there's the sound of that click. It sounds like someone's legbone snapping.

Coly Jo and I fall on our backs and smooth out our lungwind. Mister Rose makes us bust pushups. Our arms wobble and we count out twenty. All the other juvies are climbing the stairs now so they can sanitize themselves and lay up in their patch holes and wait for blackout.

Mister Rose twirls his whistle and tells us to hurry up. "Hurry up, goddamnit!" he says. "Hurry up!"

Out of the side of my eye I can see Coly Jo's face. He is smiling at me with one good eye and half his mouth.

AFTER BLACKOUT THE NOISES IN SPALDing make you feel like you're on a ship. That air sliding through the halls gets to sounding like some waves.

Coly Jo and I live in patch fourteen, just off the stairs. There are fifteen patches on your floor. You get a bunk bed, two desks with reading lights, and a chest of drawers that you got to share. I use the top two drawers and Coly Jo uses the bottom two.

They don't even give you a door, just this thing called a patch hole. Your patch hole is shaped like half of a McDonald's sign. After blackout the light in the hallway makes it glow soft and electric like a big freaky eye.

The halls are marble and everything makes those double-sounds. Even the whispers. You can hear that juvy double-lungwind and that double-choking-off and how those double-hands move. The air double-cuts through teeth and beds double-squeak through walls. And those juvy drawers double-snap when they are finished, too, like little tree branches busting.

Coly Jo is afraid of the dark and he cries. When he first got here he used to cry every night after blackout, but now he only does it a few times a week. Sometimes he tries to hide it in his pillow and his crying sounds like a dog groaning for some food.

I am looking out the window at the dead tree. The wind pulls at it so its shadow looks like a hand moving on your window. I will stay awake for the first fifteen clicks, and then it's Coly Jo's turn.

After blackout, Coly Jo walks over and turns on his reading light and throws a towel over it. That patch hole only gives as much light as it wants to. Then Coly Jo slips back in his bunk.

"Sura," he whispers.

"What."

"You awake?"

"No."

"Yes you are."

"Shhh."

"You stuck me pretty good, Sura," Coly Jo whispers.

I don't answer.

"You busted my eye," he says.

"Go to sleep."

"It swolled up."

"I had to stick a few real ones."

"I'm hip," he says. "Me, too."

"I know," I say. "You split my lip."

"You got them bony knuckles," Coly Jo says.

Coly Jo moves in his bunk again and we are quiet. I

keep watching that tree out the window. You got to wonder why they don't cut it down with some saws. A dead tree just takes up space.

"Sura," Coly Jo whispers again.

"What," I say.

"We fooled em pretty good, ain't it?"

"We fooled em," I say.

"We fooled em good," he says.

"You got all up on my back," I say.

"I'm hip," Coly Jo says. "That was gifted."

"Yeah," I whisper.

"We should bust one at the Telescope Pit tomorrow," Coly Jo says. The Telescope Pit is this drain hole just outside the gymnasium. Coly Jo and I found it one day on our way back from the hash house. We call it the Telescope Pit cause it starts out kind of big at the opening, and then those grooves gets smaller and smaller the deeper it goes, just like a telescope.

Whenever something smooth happens, like if we beat some juvies slinging craps, or if we goof on some of them and get a laugh, we go bust a piss together at the Telescope Pit. And we cross those piss streams, too, like we're some Musketeers or something.

Last week we got about four juvies with the old point-up-at-the-sky routine. All you do is stand in a spot and point up at the sky and open up your mouth so it looks like you're watching a spaceship or something. When those juvies walking by stop and look up and start mad scratching those confused domes you go, *"Got you!"* and break north with the quickness.

After Coly Jo and I goofed on those juvies like that, we broke right for that Telescope Pit and busted a long Musketeer piss right down that hole. We had some asparagus that day, too, so it smelled mad healthy.

I'll bust a piss in the Telescope Pit after I get me a rabbit, too. Sometimes I won't even stop running after the race is finished. I'll keep right on running until I get to our pit. I've busted about seven of those solo pisses so far.

"We should do it after dinner, maybe," I say.

"I'm hip," Coly Jo says.

"Go to sleep."

I turn on my side and feel my lip with my tongue. It feels like I got some Jell-O lumps all trapped in it. I feel my lip like that for a few minutes.

I keep thinking about that stick dropping down on him like it weren't attached to nothing, like it was a stick imagined from the mind of the basement. The basement's got a mind and rooms got minds. Sometimes you can hear them thinking; it sounds like old church Honeys whispering. But when you open the door there ain't no one in there and all you see is maybe some dust sliding in the light.

"You stuck me in my eyetooth, Sura," Coly Jo says and turns in the bottom bunk. "Bony-ass knuckles."

We are quiet again. I can hear the faucet dripping down the hall. Sometimes you can count that faucet for a long time and keep your head clear. I count twelve drips and turn on my side.

"Sura," Coly Jo says again.

"Damn, Coly Jo, you wanna get carped?" I whisper.

"We still gonna get out of here?" he asks.

"Yeah, man."

"When, Sura?"

"Soon as that guard goes on vacation."

"When's that?"

"Two weeks," I say.

"Two more weeks," Coly Jo says.

There ain't nothing but our lungwind now and I wonder how long those two weeks will feel with fifteen clicks of sleep a night.

Outside the night guard hits the hitchpost with his ribstick. It sounds like a pipe busting. Coly Jo shifts in his bed.

"I hate them clicks," Coly Jo says.

"I know."

"I hate em bad."

"I know," I say again.

"They don't even sound right."

"Go to sleep."

"Okay."

Coly Jo turns in his bunk again and I listen for that faucet. Sometimes Mister Rose will make a final sweep and confiscate radios or bust juvies smoking squares, and he'll pass by your patch hole like that Spalding juvy ghost you always hear about. They say you think it's Mister Rose, but then the juvy ghost shows up in your patch with all of his guts and a bunch of blue paint mad flowing out of his mouth. They say he suicided himself by drinking a bucket of blue paint. He was supposed to paint the hitchpost. You can see where he stopped painting and started drinking. They say if you look in his eyes he'll freeze you and stick his hand in your mouth and reach down your throat and crib your heart.

Tonight the halls are silent. I listen for my football game.

"Sura."

"Come on, man. Damn."

"I gotta tell you something."

Coly Jo breathes heavy for a minute like he's losing his lungwind. He gets mad spent running the stair laps. Sometimes Mister Rose has to pull him up the last flight by his belt.

"It was my birthday today, Sura," Coly Jo says.

I don't say nothing. I just lie smooth and listen for my game.

"I hit twelve."

"Happy birthday," I whisper.

"I'm twelve."

"Good."

"That's a dozen years," Coly Jo says.

"I heard you," I say.

"That's like eggs, Sura," Coly Jo says.

"Shhhhh."

Coly Jo is quiet for a minute. I will be thirteen this year. I think about how I should be messing with some of those Honeys back home on Choate Street. The ones who ride ten-speeds and stand up on the pedals so their hair jumps off their shoulders and their booty-skirts open up in the wind; the ones who will let you walk their bikes home if you're halfway smooth.

"You know what else?" Coly Jo says.

"What," I say.

"I got the tail."

"The who?"

"The tail."

"What tail?" I say.

"Off my hat—I got the tail," he says. And then I can hear him laughing into his pillow. "I got the tail," he says again. Then I hear the sound of that unbreakable comb on his Afro. It sounds like some Velcro.

"Man, you always gotta bust them naps," I say.

"I'm hip," Coly Jo says.

"Give it a rest," I say.

"I'm growin me a shag, Sura," Coly Jo says.

"Go to sleep."

"You'll see."

We are quiet again. This time it's for good. Coly Jo finally puts that unbreakable comb up. I listen for the dripping faucet and I think my ears will pick it up again cause silence is like that; those sounds will creep right up on you and fill up that emptiness. I listen for a long time, but it don't come so I watch the treehand on the window.

I will wake up Coly Jo in a while so I can get some sleep. He's breathing those deep breaths now. Tomorrow it will be my turn to go first.

HAMSTOCK BOYS CENTER IS TWO BIG-ASS rock houses, a school building, a gymnasium, the hash house, an infirmary, and a parking lot (my rabbit line), where they'll walk you in circles if you get carped enough. And they'll have you walk those circles smaller and smaller until you're practically stepping on your own toes and it feels like you got some pennies stacked in the floors of your shoes. And they'll make you count out with each circle, too.

My rabbit line cuts right in front of this old two-lane highway that curves sharp and gray like a dead snake and disappears into the sky.

All the buildings are made out of square stones, and when it rains those stones turn dark and shiny.

There is also a twenty-foot fence with those jagged links across the top. It ain't electrified, and you can shake it so it sounds like you got some quarters in your pockets, but it'll cut you up like paper if you get stuck on those top links. The fence makes a square around Hamstock and all you can see besides that highway are some old, torn-up bean fields.

One juvy got himself stuck to the top of the fence and had to get mad stitches.

Sometimes when we're in the parking lot for gut drill a juvy'll walk up to that fence and put his hands on it like you put your hands on one of those department store windows. You only get a minute between the pushups and situps, but for that minute you think you can reach right out and touch that bean field, like you can hold some dirt in your hand. But you got to be careful cause if you touch the fence too much Mister Tully will know and he'll find a reason to carp you.

Mister Tully runs gut drill. He's got a raspberry spot on his face and he fought in a war and he's got those eyes that let you know when to keep away from the fence.

We are standing in line at the infirmary, just outside Nurse Rushing's office. We are facing the wall and holding red lice combs. They make you face the wall when you stand in line for shit. They think it stops juvies from chucking.

I am standing next to Coly Jo. He didn't sanitize himself this morning and he smells like a can of horseflies. He's been carrying the tail of his squirrel-skin cap around in his pocket. His hand's been fidgeting in that pocket all day.

Coly Jo got six months for breaking into people's houses. He never did nothing to them, never cribbed or vandaled shit. He just liked to watch them sleep.

He told me how he'd watch the moonlight creep right

over a face, and how that moonlight would sometimes make a face change and look old. He said he would watch for those changes and then when their breathing would shift and they'd start to wake up he would creep out through a window.

Sometimes I think Coly Jo watches me sleep, but I can't tell for sure cause waking up can be mad confusing. There are those times when you don't know if you're still in a dream. You get that funny dizzy feeling like when you been walking on some railroad tracks for a long time. The only thing you can go by is the light.

Sometimes I dream that Coly Jo is watching me sleep, but then I wake up and hear him breathing like he's in a cave and I know he is sleeping and the light changes from that blue dream light to the color of the light in patch fourteen, which is like the non-light of a gas station when it's closed.

Coly Jo is next in line. You can see Nurse Rushing at her desk, pushing through Dorsey Payne's nappy hair. Dorsey Payne got caught trying to crib a Thanksgiving turkey out of an unmarked cop car. They gave him four months with good behavior. He would've gotten six weeks if it weren't no cop car. He is sitting at a chair next to the nurse and his mouth keeps seizing up so you can see his gums. Nurse Rushing has found too much of the bad stuff and she sends him to the next room to have his head shaved. You can hear that skullrazor buzzing loud and clear.

Coly Jo is next. When he walks his feet are slow and he's still got that fire-hand. When he sits down Nurse

Rushing asks him to take his other hand out of his pocket. I can hear her talking to Coly Jo and him going "Yes ma'am." She is telling him that she has found lice. She tells him to go into the next room and he says "Yes ma'am" again and then a door closes and there is the sound of that skullrazor. So much for that shag he was growing.

She calls me over and I take a seat next to her desk. Nurse Rushing is a white Honey and she's got those smooth hands and that good medicine smell. Sometimes I think she likes me cause her eyes slide to the left like she might have certain thoughts about my sexiness. But you never know about that stuff. If you get to thinking about those smooth hands too much it'll just about drive you to busting a sex pole.

She starts to comb through my hair.

"You still puttin those chemicals in your hair, Sura?" she asks.

"No ma'am," I say.

"That stuff's not for your kind of hair."

"Yes ma'am."

"It'll burn your scalp if you keep messin with it."

She starts to comb through the back of my hair and I try to look down her nurse's uniform. There's something about a nurse's uniform that'll make you feel mad sexy. It's all of that white material moving over the skin. That white material can get closer than a hand can.

Sometimes I'll think about Nurse Rushing taking that uniform off and folding it over a chair. You'd be surprised how sexy the right kind of Honey folding some clothes over a chair can be. I might ask her out if I had the time.

"Sura," Nurse Rushing says suddenly, "you better put those eyes back where they belong."

I look at my hands.

"You must wanna get carped."

"No ma'am," I say.

We are silent now and she is working through the other side of my head. That comb feels like a bird pecking at my scalp. I hope I don't got no lice. I've heard how they'll eat away at your skull and grub up your brain. You got to be careful about that shit.

"You're clean," Nurse Rushing says, and drops the comb in the junk can.

On my way back to Spalding I can see Petey Sessoms standing under the dead tree. His hands are fists and he is looking down at the ground like he's sick. Hodge is standing in front of Petey Sessoms, holding a spoon that he cribbed from the hash house.

Petey Sessoms is one of the strongest juvies in Spalding. He's got those back muscles that pop out when he climbs the Alabama rope in gym class. The Alabama rope goes clear up to the ceiling. Petey Sessoms is the only juvy who can climb all the way to the top. Sometimes after juvy pound he'll set two or three tenths on the rafters.

Things started to go bad for Petey Sessoms when juvies found out that he couldn't keep his blood down. One day in his patch he was showing some of us how to use chocko sticks. One of his boys had sneaked them to him in a package of comic books. He accidentally busted himself in the knee and it opened up with the quickness and wouldn't stop bleeding. Mister Rose called the infirmary and had Petey Sessoms hauled away on a body plate. And he mad confiscated those chocko sticks, too.

When Petey Sessoms got back from the infirmary he told his patch mate how he was a hebofeeliac and his patch mate spread that around the hash house so quick it was like he got paid to do it. I swear, at Hamstock if they catch you with a paper cut on your finger they'll walk right up to you and pull on that finger and make that cut open up wide.

I guess that's why Petey Sessoms can climb that Alabama rope so quick: you got to be strong to protect your blood. That's why he's got those muscles popping out of his back.

So after all the juvies found out that he couldn't keep his blood down, Hodge kept talking about how he was going to buffalo Petey Sessoms and show all the other juvies how Mister Alabama Rope weren't so tough after all.

If you buffalo another juvy it means you make him climb the dead tree in front of Spalding. If you're getting buffaloed you can either chuck or climb right up there and sit in those branches for everyone to see.

I don't think Boo and Hodge really know what buffalo means cause I borrowed Mister Rose's pocket dictionary at study box one night and it didn't say nothing about making someone climb no tree. It just talked about the animal and how it is a wild ox and how it hangs out in the Mississippi River. But they use that word anyway and so do all of the other juvies.

So Petey Sessoms is standing there in front of the dead tree. He is looking down at the ground and you can see Hodge's spoon catching the light. Some other juvies are coming up behind me from the infirmary.

Hodge throws his spoon down in the dirt. Petey Sessoms looks over his shoulder at us and then up at the dead tree and then back at us. I want Petey Sessoms to forget that he is a hebofeeliac. I want him to lower his shoulder and throw Hodge up against that tree.

Hodge takes his shirt off and he's got a chest like a man's chest and those muscles are wide and mad thick and go shiny in the sun.

I look up at the third floor of Spalding and Boo's dented head appears in a patch window and you can see his white eyes. The other juvies have caught up to me now.

Petey Sessoms looks up at that window and then back to us and then up at that window again. Then Petey Sessoms takes two steps toward the tree. I hear a juvy behind me say "Do him, Petey, do him" through his teeth. But Petey just looks at the tree, grabs the lowest branch, and starts climbing.

Once he reaches the third branch, he sits in that tree and some birds fly out and disappear over Spalding. Hodge puts his shirt back on and bends down and picks up that spoon. He uses the end of it to carve another notch next to his initials. The bottom of that tree's got so many initials and notches you'd think wild dogs creep into Hamstock at night and grub on the trunk.

As we walk toward Spalding, Hodge pretends not to notice us, but once we get close to the tree he shakes his head and goes, "Got me another one, Sham. Got me another one."

No one knows who Sham is, but Hodge will sometimes talk to him like that.

One time this juvy who was transferred from St. Chuck's heard Hodge talking like that and he thought he was slick and called *Hodge* Sham. That night Hodge set that juvy's head on fire while he was sleeping and burned off half his Afro. No one said a word, though, and that new juvy had a burn on his head for a long time and had to wrap it in some hospital rags.

Things got so bad between him and Hodge that he begged to be transferred back to St. Chuck's. They wouldn't do it, though. They sent him to Kankakee instead. That's where they got that lucky river. If you escape you can snatch on to some driftwood and float away.

When I look up to the third branch, Petey Sessoms is staring at his feet. He will not raise his eyes to meet mines.

It's after blackout. Coly Jo and I count four clicks and creep out of our patch and down the fire stairs. You got to use your best Indian feet when you're on the fire stairs or Fat Rick will hear you and page security with the quickness.

Fat Rick does the Spalding beat every night. Most of the time he's too busy drinking that cough syrup and winds up falling out at his desk. You got to wait about six clicks before he's out, though.

We are standing in the sweet spot in the basement and Mister Rose has one of those skin flicks on. The Honey in that skin flick is mad crying out like she's being attacked by some boogymonsters.

It's funny how those skin flicks are like that. If you *watch* a skin flick it looks like a man and a woman rubbing all up against each other, like those sexy parts of the blood are mad cooking. And those arms and legs are flying out and they got those eyes like they're praying. But if you just *listen* to it it sounds all crazy and bugged-out. When you *listen* to a skin flick it sounds like a Honey is getting a spike all nailed into her hand with a hammer or something. And that music is mad for the birds, too, like someone made it up on one of those fake-ass Casio piano boards.

Coly Jo keeps rocking back and forth with that hand on his belly while that Honey in the skin flick is crying out *Oooohhhhh* and *Aaaahhhhh* and *Noooo* and *Yessss* and *Harder, harder!* and shit.

This is our third time down here after blackout. Each time Coly Jo gets to rocking, his hand slips over his belly and turns into a fire-hand and his lungwind starts cooking. The light is off and we can't even see each other. I got Coly Jo by his belt just in case that rocking of his gets out of control.

Sometimes you can hear Mister Rose's voice mixed in with the skin flick. He ain't really saying nothing, though. He's just making a bunch of non-words like *Hock!* and *Zam!* And he keeps saying those non-words over and over, too. You don't even want to *picture* what he's doing up in his room. He's probably all naked and shit. And those shark eyes are probably mad popping out of his head.

I pull Coly Jo by his belt. "Come on, man," I say. Coly Jo is still mad rocking. Last week I rocked back and forth while Coly Jo held my belt.

After those Hocks and Zams start to get played out, Coly Jo stops rocking and we put our Indian feet back on and climb those fire stairs.

Fat Rick knows how to sleep so it looks like he's reading a book. Those folds in his neck are mad heavy.

IF YOU STARE AT A MAN'S HEAD LONG enough it starts to look like a hunk of wax, especially if that head is bald and kind of yellow. I'm sitting in front of Deacon Bob Fly and he's bumping at the gums about something but all I can think about is his head and how you could melt a bunch of candles in a pot and scoop out that warm wax and make his head.

Deacon Bob Fly is my Path Mentor. He probably drives one of those non-smooth American rides that don't even got no hoody. Or if his ride does got a hoody you can bet that that hoody is all plastic and shit—probably an Olds or one of those gray Ford Fairmonts with the AM radio and pleather interior. There ain't nothing sadder than a pleather interior.

Sometimes you can get to looking at someone and know what kind of ride he's got. Usually a smooth pair of shoes means a smooth ride. You'd be surprised how often that plays out like that. Slider told me about that when I started clipping hoodies.

You meet with your Path Mentor twice a week: once in the morning and once at night after study box.

Deacon Bob Fly's face is always mad sweating like he's been in the sun too long. And he always sports that same mint-green shirt with the butterfly collar. I guess he's one of those undercover priest types who hide the little white neck flap. You got to watch out for those guys. They're like those cops who dress up as junkies and hang out in the parking lots and then throw that shoulder lock on you when you're sizing up some hoodies.

What's freaky is that Deacon Bob Fly don't even talk about *God* all that much. You'd think he'd get to bumping at the gums about it all the time, but he don't.

Once in a while he'll throw around a story about this fisherman whose family is starving to death and how that fisherman goes out on this holy river in a rowboat to catch some trout. He don't have no faith and he curses and chews tobacco and goes to the dog track and drinks Mad Dog 20/20, so God won't let him have no trout. And then his boat sinks and his family starves and he gets grubbed up by a one-eyed goonfish. The way Deacon Bob Fly tells the story you'd think he's more interested in the *goonfish* than in God. He gets mad descriptive about that goonfish.

Today Deacon Bob Fly is showing me a picture out of a Curious George book. Curious George is at the circus and he's sitting on a bench in front of three cages. One cage holds a bear, one holds an ostrich, and one holds a kangaroo moms with a kid in her pouch.

Curious George has stripped all of his clothes off and stuck them over the other end of the bench by his party horn. Curious George has about the saddest face you've ever seen on a monkey. His arms are just hanging there between his legs and his back is all slumping.

Deacon Bob Fly reads the words above the picture in one of those slow voices. He reads how the circus director is mad pissed at Curious George and how he won't use little monkeys who don't do like they're told. Then Deacon Bob Fly reads how the director tells Curious George that he can't be in the circus show and how they're going to send his ass home. Curious George has to sit on a bench all by himself, and nobody even looks at him. Then Deacon Bob Fly reads about how George is all sorry and mad crying about what he did, but how it's too late cause he's already messed everything up.

Deacon Bob Fly pushes the book in front of me and drums his fingers on the desk. When he drums his fingers like that you know he's about to ask you something. Sometimes he'll get to drumming those fingers for a long time and you hope he'll just keep right on drumming them for the rest of the session.

"So, what do you think, Sura?" Deacon Bob Fly says.

"About what, Deacon Bob," I say.

He wipes his face and shifts in his chair.

"About the picture," he says, settling into a new position. Deacon Bob Fly's got mad positions that he likes to settle in.

"It's a picture for kids, Deacon Bob," I say.

"I know that, Sura," he says, "but what do you think?"

"I ain't no kid, Deacon Bob," I say.

"But how does it make you *feel?*" he asks.

Deacon Bob Fly is always asking me how things make

me *feel*. One day he ate a big piece of chocolate cake in front of me and took those mad slow bites and moved his mouth around like it was the best piece of chocolate cake ever made. Then he asked me how it made me *feel* when he did that. I told him that it didn't make me *feel* nothing but that he might *feel* like getting himself a cold glass of milk and some vanilla ice cream cause chocolate cake and a glass of cold milk and some vanilla ice cream all taste pretty smooth together. Especially if it's about sixty-five degrees out and that sun is dropping and there are some smooth colors in the sky. When I told him all of that, Deacon Bob Fly just shook his head and said *Sura, Sura* like he was saying it to his butterfly collar.

But sometimes you got to play his *feel* game so that he'll think you're making reform.

"Does it make you want to laugh?" Deacon Bob Fly asks, pointing at the picture.

"No, Deacon Bob," I say.

"Shout?" he asks.

"No, Deacon Bob."

"Does it make you feel unhinged?" he asks. I try to picture what it would be like to be unhinged but all I can see is a big door stuck to my body.

"No, Deacon Bob," I say again.

"Talk to me, Sura."

"I don't know what to say, Deacon Bob."

"You don't have to call me 'Deacon Bob' so much," he says. "Not in here."

"Okay, Deacon Bob," I say. Then I realize what I've just said and I go, "Sorry . . . Sorry."

We are silent for a moment. You can hear his desk clock clipping time. That's some mad quiet silence to hear clock parts like that.

"If you were Curious George, what would you do?" he asks. "Would you play on that horn?"

"I can't play no horn," I say.

"Just pretend," he says. "If you *could* play the horn, would you play it?"

"No," I say.

"Why?"

"I don't know," I say.

"Tell me why," Deacon Bob Fly says.

"Cause it would just piss em off."

"Why, Sura?"

"Cause, man . . . ," I say.

"Because why?"

"Cause, man, it would be like some juvy getting out of here and . . ."

"And what?"

"And then showing up a few days later sporting a nice windbreaker and smoking a square right outside the fence, and . . ."

"And what, Sura?"

"And we would all run up to him so we could see if he had some wristbands on . . ."

"Go on," he says.

"But he wouldn't show em to us and he'd have some bones in his pocket and he'd be blowin that smoke right through the fence . . ."

Deacon Bob Fly starts to drum his fingers on the desk

again. For some reason, I start to hear the music from my electronic football game. But I hear it in my mind and I know it's in my mind cause it's got that deep hallway double-sound like Boo and Hodge are playing it under some covers down in their patch.

"So what would you do?"

"Huh?" I say.

"If you were Curious George, what would you do?" Deacon Bob Fly asks.

"Man, that's a kid's book."

It sounds like my voice has suddenly changed, like there is some food in my throat. There's a part of your voice that you don't recognize sometimes, and the only way you know that it's yours is cause you can feel those vibrations buzzing strange in your throatbox.

"Answer the question, Sura," Deacon Bob Fly says. His face is mad sweating now. I don't say nothing and I am making fists on my lap.

"Go on," Deacon Bob Fly says. "Say it."

I stare down at the book. That look on Curious George's face is about the saddest look you've ever seen on a monkey. And there ain't nothing too happy about that bear or that ostrich or that kangaroo moms and her kid, either. It's even sadder than this picture that was in the YMCA room where Mazzy and I stayed last year for a while. Mazzy is my moms, but I call her Mazzy. She's a famous dancer. She calls me by my last name and I call her by her first name. It works out pretty smooth. Once in a while she'll call me by my first name but she only does that when she gets sad or pissed off. She had me when she was fifteen. She had to drop out of high school and get a job at a grocery store. She don't like to call me by my first name cause that's my pops's first name, too. She's got it tattooed on her ankle.

When I get out of here I'm going to get me a tattoo. This guy around my way does it for fifty bones. I'm going to have him draw a hoody on my left shoulder; my left shoulder is smoother-looking than my right shoulder. My right shoulder's got all of those marks on it you get when they burn you so you don't get polo and chicken pops and shit like that.

When I get that tattoo I'm going to cut the sleeves off of my T-shirts, too, so those Honeys on Choate Street will see it and get that flavor up in their mouths.

Anyway, that picture in our YMCA room was a picture of Jesus holding this blind baby. You could tell that the baby was blind cause there was nothing but some light where his eyes were supposed to be—no eye dots or nothing.

Before we moved out of that room I took a magic marker and drew some shades for that baby. I couldn't stand to look at that empty light in his eyes no more. Even Mazzy thought that picture was sad.

Deacon Bob Fly is drumming his fingers again. His face is sweating worse than ever.

"Say what you want to say, Sura," he says.

I want to tell him how I'd open up those cages and set the animals free and blow loud on that party horn so they'd run off, and I want to yell it out so the vibrations from my throatbox make his butterfly collar fly up, but I don't. I just sit there and watch my fists shake. I keep thinking about that blind baby and staying in the YMCA and my electronic football game and that sad monkey face and Coly Jo's non-birthday and Petey Sessoms climbing up in that dead tree.

My face is wet now and I don't even know why. Big, dumb Honey tears.

"Good, Sura. Good . . . ," Deacon Bob Fly says, for some reason. His wax head shines yellow and ugly.

I will be thirteen this year, I think to myself. I will be thirteen this year, and when I get out of here those Honeys on Choate Street better watch out, goddamnit.

COLY JO'S GOT A BALDY. YOU CAN SEE THE lumps on his skull. His head is mad flat, too, and when I laugh at him he goes, "C'mon, Sura, c'mon, man." I ain't laughing with sound, though. I'm just using my face and my eyes and I can't stop.

We are in study box and Coly Jo keeps trying to bust me in the shins under the table.

Study box is on the main level of Spalding. There are five hash tables with four chairs at each table. The walls are whiter than paper and if you look at them too long they'll make you sleepy. Mister Rose sits in the half-couch reading his word book like an old man.

The only other thing in the room besides the tables, chairs, and half-couch is the iron radiator. If you get carped for the smallest thing Mister Rose will stick you in pushup position with your feet propped up on that radiator, even if it's hissing and spitting out that nasty water. And he'll keep you in that position so your arms start shaking and your lungwind seizes up. But I can't resist snapping on Coly Jo's baldy.

"Nugget head," I say.

"Cut it, man."

"Raisin dome."

Mister Rose looks up and we are quiet. I stare down at my math book and Coly Jo tries to kick me again. After a minute all you can hear are the lights buzzing.

I'm busting some math digits and Coly Jo's got his vowel book open. Coly Jo can't read yet. He knows the alphabet, though, and sometimes you can hear him singing that alphabet song to himself in our patch. He can do the high parts, too. It gets to be kind of smooth sometimes.

Coly Jo's problem is that he can't put letters together so they make sense. The letters in that book are so big that they can only fit about five on each page. Coly Jo traces those big letters with his fingers. It looks like he's feeling something small and dead.

Coly Jo is in a special slate docket and he tells me how the teacher talks with a slow voice and how that slow voice makes those words seem longer and longer. But I know Coly Jo is smart about shit. Those books can't bill how you can sneak into somebody's house while they're in it, or how you can get that private color up in your eyes. That stuff takes special smarts—smarts with the quickness, as Slider says.

I'm trying to keep all of that math in my head. It's the one subject at slate docket that I don't mind too much. Some numbers are mad sexy. Take the number 3, for instance: if you turn that number on its side it starts to look like a nice set of Honey bosoms, and if you draw some dots on those bosoms you have yourself some titties to go with it. That's how math can get sometimes. Once in a while I'll just sit in class and draw those sideways 3's. And I'll add some titty dots and I'll draw a face on it and some legs and arms, and soon enough I'll get to thinking about those Honeys back home on Choate Street. The number 7 is pretty good for arms and legs.

Math's definitely got its smooth parts.

Sometimes you can get to thinking about certain types of numbers and use those thoughts to fill up your head, but it only lasts so long, and then other thoughts start to creep into your mind the way dogs will creep into a room when there's food on the floor.

For some reason, I keep picturing the side of the house where Mazzy stays. She stays with this man called Flintlock. I don't know what he does or where he's from. In a letter Mazzy told me he's got a bunch of tattoos all up and down his arms.

A couple of weeks ago I looked up "flintlock" in Mister Rose's word book and it said it was some kind of lock you stick on a gun.

In the same letter Mazzy sent a picture of Flintlock's house. It's gray with this old-ass aluminum siding and it's about the size of a Fotomat. There's a gravel driveway and a tetherball pole that don't even got no ball on the string and a busted window with a plastic garbage sack taped over it.

I'm trying to add some fractions, but all I keep seeing is that aluminum siding on Flintlock's house and how those rusty slates look like they're about to fall off.

Boo and Hodge are at the far table. They keep passing

notes back and forth. Boo is smiling and when he smiles that harelip sticks right up on his tooth. When Boo smiles like that you know he's planning something.

One night Boo and Hodge packed some soap in a pillow sack and slipped into a new juvy's patch and beat him with that soap sack. That's why they give us those soap flakes now instead of bars.

That juvy sleeps with his eyes open now. He's always got those puffy eyes and he wound up in Hamstock cause he took a bow and arrows to school one day and shot at teachers from the roof. He didn't hit no one, though. And the arrows had plastic tips. But they gave him eight months for it.

If someone busted me up with a soap sack I don't know what I'd do. I ain't never killed a kid before. I busted a kid in the head with a can of Sterno once, but that's cause he cribbed some of my hoodies: two Benzos and a Jag. Those are the smoothest ones on the market, too. I could've gotten some pretty thick bones for them. At least fifty. So I found out he cribbed them and sold them to some kid across town.

One night I saw him slinging craps against the wall of the bowling alley and I found that can of Sterno in the parking lot. I walked over to him with those quiet Indian feet and busted him in the back of his head. He fell up against that wall and slid down it like one of those birds that fly into a window cause they think it's the sky. That kid walked with a hospital rag on his head for a week and learned to stay away from me and my hoodies. That's the closest I ever came to killing a kid.

Mister Rose leaves the room for a moment, and when the door closes, Boo pulls Coly Jo's squirrel-skin cap out of his pocket and puts it on his head. Coly Jo is still tracing those vowels with his fingers.

Boo starts to make smooching sounds and I look and I can see his muscled-up lips and how they are meant for Coly Jo. Coly Jo gets that fire-hand again and then he looks up and watches Boo and Hodge. Those smooches get louder and louder. Coly Jo closes his book and looks over at the empty half-couch where Mister Rose was sitting and then back to Boo and Hodge. That color is starting to mad rise up in his eyes.

"Don't do it, Coly Jo," I whisper. "Don't do it."

Coly Jo just stares at them. His fire-hand turns into a fist. That color in his eyes is mad strange. It don't even got a name.

FOR GRUB TODAY WE GOT MEAT AND corn. That's about the best meal they give you at Hamstock, especially when they throw some potatoes on your plate, too, and serve it up hot.

We are holding our dicks over the Telescope Pit. When we piss we make those Musketeer crosses and that steam rises right up out of the ground. The sun is starting to fall out and the sky is clouded and has that dirty-water color.

Coly Jo is smiling cause he is full and he is still busting his piss. Coly Jo will sometimes smile for fifteen or twenty minutes after he grubs, and for that time he'll look like somebody else. He's usually got that run-down non-look on his face, his mouth straight like someone drew it on with a pencil. But some of that hash house food and a good Musketeer piss over the Telescope Pit will get that smile up. We zip up and head back to Spalding.

"That food was good, ain't it, Sura?" he says.

"I'm hip."

"It was hot."

"It was," I say.

"You take seconds?" he asks.

"Yep," I say.

"I took thirds," Coly Jo says.

"I saw you," I say.

"You didn't take thirds," he says.

"Didn't want thirds," I say.

"I wanted fourths," Coly Jo says, still smiling.

"You're fat as hell, too," I say.

"I'm hip," he says.

"You should try to slim down."

"Why?" he asks.

"Cause," I say.

"Cause why?"

"You know why."

Then we are quiet for a moment. Some juvies are running past us from the hash house and their sneakers sound like brooms on the concrete. Most of them are going to play three clicks' worth of floor hockey before blackout.

"I know why," Coly Jo says after everyone runs past us.

"Good."

"It's in case we gotta run, right? You don't want me slowin us down, right?"

I am watching how those juvies are running, how their arms and legs are fighting through the air as if those three clicks' worth of free time is the most important thing they know.

"Ain't I right, Sura?" Coly Jo asks. "You want me to be quick," he says.

"You need to get over that fence, too," I say.

"I knew it," Coly Jo says.

"And you're gonna have to get new clothes if you keep it up."

"I knew it," Coly Jo says again.

All of a sudden you can hear those smooching sounds again. Boo Boxfoot is sitting in front of the dead tree, making lips at Coly Jo. He looks like an old man sitting there, like he's walked for a long time and now is laying up for some rest. He's sporting the squirrel-skin cap.

The word on Boo Boxfoot is that he blinded this old lady around his way by busting her in the head with a crowbar. He'll probably be at Hamstock until he turns sixteen. There are only a few juvies at Hamstock with those full sentences like that. Around here they call that a Sweet-tooth Clip cause you don't get out until your Sweet Sixteenth birthday.

It's kind of funny how Boo and Hodge won't mess with me. I think it's cause I beat Boo in a race my third week here. I dusted his ass good, too. I couldn't even hear his lungwind behind me for the last fifty feet. He still makes me rent that night table, though. But he keeps it private, just between me and him.

With the light fading, the only parts of Boo's face you can see are his eyes and his front tooth.

"Shucks," Coly Jo says. That grub smile falls right off of his face.

"Just keep walkin," I say.

"Dag, Sura," Coly Jo says. "Dag."

"Just keep walkin, man," I say.

"I ain't goin up in that tree, Sura."

We reach the tree and Boo is standing now. Those

smooching noises are louder now and sound like some Styrofoam rubbing together. Boo stops smooching and steps in front of Coly Jo.

"Coly Jo is a hoe," Boo says.

Coly Jo just stands there.

"Hoe-hoe-hoe, whaddaya know?" Boo says, smiling.

Boo likes to rhyme like that. He won't usually say much, but when he speaks, those rhymes come out smooth and quick like he's been thinking about them.

"I want my hat, Boo," Coly Jo says, pulling his pants up.

"Hi-hoe, Coly Jo," Boo says.

Coly Jo just stands there and stares at Boo. Boo stares back at Coly Jo.

"You keep tryin to punk me and I ain't no punk," Coly Jo says. He's got those fire-hands again.

"Be cool, Coly Jo," I say.

"I ain't no punk," Coly Jo says again, staring at Boo.

I can't tell whether or not the color is up in his eyes cause the sun is falling out so fast. It is one of those fall-outs that just creeps up on you and goes black.

Now Boo is smooching his lips right in front of Coly Jo's face. I look up and I can see Hodge looking out of his patch window.

"Be cool, Coly Jo."

"I ain't climbin no tree, Sura," Coly Jo says, staring back at Boo.

"Use your head, man," I say.

"I ain't climbin nothin."

Boo continues smooching closer and closer to Coly Jo's

face and I think he will get so close that he will kiss him.

"He can beat me, Sura, but I ain't climbin no tree," Coly Jo says, breathing hard now.

Suddenly the night guard starts to walk toward us. It's like he's been imagined by the falling dark. He is old and has a folded-up white face and when he walks he twirls his ribstick in his hand.

"Evenin, fellas," he says.

"Evenin, Mister," we all say. No one knows the night guard's real name, so we just call him Mister.

"Everything okay?" he asks, looking at all three of us.

"Yes sir, Mister," Boo says.

"Yes sir, Mister," Coly Jo and I say.

"That's good," the night guard says. "We gotta keep stuff up to snuff around here."

We are all quiet. Boo takes a step back.

"It's gettin kinda late for carpin," the night guard says. "I don't care too much for carpin a juvy at the end of the day. It's like eatin a wet sandwich . . ."

"Yes sir, Mister," Boo says.

"Yes sir, Mister," Coly Jo and I say. The night guard picks some stuff out of his teeth and twirls his ribstick a few times.

"Won't be no chuckin tonight," the night guard says.

All three of us go "Yes sir, Mister" again. This time I say it first and Coly Jo and Boo follow.

"You best get inside, then," the night guard says. Boo slowly turns and Coly Jo just stands there until I poke him in the back. "Go on now," the night guard says.

We start to walk toward the entrance of Spalding. If

you're close enough you can hear how the night guard twirls his ribstick.

Boo is ahead of us and he is stroking the back of Coly Jo's cap. Before he opens the door to Spalding he turns back to us and stares at Coly Jo.

"Fat hoe can't climb no tree no ways," he says and turns and enters.

"I ain't no hoe and I ain't no punk," Coly Jo says.

After Boo is inside I look up.

Hodge is still framed in the dark light of his patch window.

It's just before blackout. That patch hole light is starting to go soft and electric. We are laying up in our bunks. Once in a while Coly Jo and I will just lay up like that for a click or two and talk. But you can only do that for about two clicks cause Mister Rose will have you busting stair laps if he hears you on his blackout sweep.

Sometimes talking to Coly Jo can be smoother than talking to Deacon Bob Fly and his yellow head. A lot smoother.

But sometimes Coly Jo will get to bumping at the gums about this game he used to play with his boys called Get the Flaptooth. It was a trick they would play on this old man who owned a socks and slipper shop. Coly Jo and his boys would hide out and wait for him to close up his shop. That old man had to latch up about four different locks. When he would finish pulling his gate down they'd set off some firecrackers in a junk can and the old man would snap out with the quickness.

Coly Jo said that the old man would take his shirt off and start twisting it all around his arm like a blood-stopper. And sometimes he would climb under somebody's ride and start mad shouting out "Fire in the hole!" and shit like that.

Coly Jo said there was this one time when the old man got so scared that he just sat down and put his face between his legs and covered his head with the top of that same junk can they'd set off the firecrackers in. That's about the saddest thing you'll see a grown man do. Especially an *old* grown man.

They called him the Flaptooth cause he would get this mad bugged-out look on his face and his mouth would open up and this one old tooth would show. Coly Jo said that that tooth was all long and snaggly.

It's kind of messed up, how Coly Jo and his boys would do that. All that shit with firecrackers just to see a funny-looking tooth.

Slider always told me not to mess with old people. You think cause they're all bow-legged and creaky in the joints that they would be easy targets. But those old guys will surprise you and pull out a gun with the quickness. Some of them carry two guns. They got one on their hip and another one by their anklebone. They don't got time to be messing with kids.

When Coly Jo starts telling those Get the Flaptooth stories I just let his voice fade out like some TV snow. And sometimes that TV snow will fill up my head for two whole clicks.

But Coly Jo ain't talked about the Flaptooth in the

longest. I kept telling him what Slider told me, and he kept going, "For real, Sura? For real?"

So I tune back in now. As long as we get the talk finished before Mister Rose's blackout sweep, I don't mind.

"Sura," he says.

"Huh."

"You ever try talkin to a dog?" he asks.

"No," I say. "Have you?"

"Yeah."

"Why?" I ask.

"Cause dogs know stuff that folks don't."

"Like what?" I ask.

"They know when you afraid," Coly Jo says.

I don't answer that. I just lie quiet. That's what I do when Coly Jo starts throwing his four tenths of knowledge around. If I'm quiet I know he'll keep right on talking.

"And they know when you got some food on you," he adds. "I had some gum hided in my shoe once and this dog knew," he says.

"Damn," I say.

"I had it hided right on my toe," Coly Jo says.

"And he knew," I say.

"I'm hip," Coly Jo says. "His name was Banjo."

"That's a smooth name," I say.

"I'm hip," Coly Jo says again.

"I never had a dog," I say.

"Me either," Coly Jo says.

Then we are quiet for a minute. You can almost hear how Coly Jo is about to say something. He keeps stopping up his lungwind and then letting it out, like he's got to hold that air inside him to put those thoughts together.

"There's this dog around my way who knows kung fu," Coly Jo says.

"Stop, man," I say.

"For God," Coly Jo says. "I ain't lyin."

"That's crazy, man," I say.

"For God, Sura," he says again.

"Damn, that's crazy."

I'm laughing now. That's about the funniest thing I've heard since I've been at Hamstock. I picture a dog throwing a jump-kick with one of those kung fu housecoats on. You hear about dogs driving golf carts and delivering groceries and shit like that. But you don't hear about no dogs doing *kung fu*.

"He blasted this dude in the chest once," Coly Jo says.

Now I'm laughing so hard I think I'm going to fall off my bunk.

"*Blasted* him," Coly Jo says.

"Stop, man," I say.

"For God, Sura."

Man, my chest is almost seizing up on me. I have that chocolate milk belly, too. That's what Slider and I call it when we get to laughing at some boogies in someone's nose—that chocolate milk belly. It feels all smooth and open.

"Dogs got brains in their noses, too," Coly Jo says.

"They got that 'nose knowledge,'" I say, still mad laughing, still picturing that kung fu dog.

"I'm hip," Coly Jo says.

Then the first blackout click busts. That chocolate milk

belly closes right up. Everything goes mad silent. You can't even hear the hallway. It's almost like the hallway's stopped breathing.

"Sura," Coly Jo says.

"We only got one more click," I say.

"I know, I know," he says.

"Go head," I say.

"When I would glide through folks' houses I likeded if they had a dog."

"You musta liked gettin that ass bit, too," I say.

"I likeded talkin to em."

"You can't talk to no dog," I say.

"Yes you can, Sura," Coly Jo says. "You can talk to em with your eyes."

"I thought dogs was colorblind," I say.

"They *listen* to your eyes."

I don't say nothing for a minute, but I want to keep talking for some reason, so I go, "That's pretty smooth."

"I would say, 'Hey dog, what's up man?' and that dog would just look at me with his eyes and say, 'Come on in. I ain't gonna bite you.'" Coly Jo's voice starts to go all quiet and soft. "And sometimes he would get to snuffin my hand," Coly Jo says, "and he would listen to my eyes and then I would start to pet him."

Now we are quiet. I think that our talk might be over so I turn over in my bunk and try and get comfortable. Those patch bunks can get mad stiff sometimes. Once in a while you got to pull your mattress down and beat it with your fist so it softens up.

"Sura?" Coly Jo says.

"Huh."

"When I get outta here I'ma get me a dog."

"Yeah?"

"On the strength," he says.

"I'm gonna get me some Honeys," I say, but I say that mostly to myself. I picture some Honeys flipping their booty-skirts around in front of the bowling alley. Even though they never really do that, I like to picture it.

"That's the first thing I'ma do," Coly Jo says.

"What kinda dog?"

"I ain't hip," he says.

"One of those kung fu dogs?" I say.

"One that talks good with his eyes. Them blueticks got some pretty tough eyes."

"What are you gonna name him?" I ask.

"Jewel."

"That's a smooth name," I say.

"Yeah," Coly Jo says. "That's what they called my moms."

"She left?" I ask.

"Yeah," Coly Jo says. But he says it so you can barely hear it. Then he goes even softer and says, "She dead, Sura."

I don't say nothing for a minute. That's a mad hard thing to talk about. After hearing something like that you can forget about getting that chocolate milk belly up again.

Then Coly Jo moves in his bunk a little and goes, "She sleeped to death." And when he stops moving we don't say nothing for a minute. I feel like I should say something, so after that minute I go, "Man."

"Man" is the only thing I can think of to say. You never

hear about someone's moms dying like that. You hear about other stuff, about how someone will get sick from cancer or get in a car crash or suicide themself with floor cleaner and shit, but you don't never hear about no one *sleeping* to death. You just don't hear about that.

Then I say it again just like that. I go, "Man," and we are quiet.

"I putted her hand in some water, too," Coly Jo says. "I putted it right in a bucket, but she wouldn't wake up," he says. "That water trick don't work so hot."

I don't say nothing back this time. I just close my eyes and let things even out in my head. It's kind of funny how Coly Jo calls breaking into people's houses "gliding through." The way he talks about it makes it sound like he's a ghost, like he can just turn into some water drops and get through the crack in a window. I guess the way you talk about clipping hoodies is kind of like that. You don't say *cribbing* hoodies. Using the word "clipping" makes it sound pretty smooth.

That stuff about dogs listening with their eyes is pretty smooth, too. You can *think* about that shit. You can even *picture* that. You can watch yourself petting a dog or throwing a stick with a dog. You can even picture a *kung fu* dog sporting one of those kung fu housecoats. I saw this one kung fu flick where this guy's housecoat had powers in it and if he threw it over you it would *freeze* you. After he threw it over this one guy and the guy froze up, the guy with the housecoat started doing all of this snake style and tiger style and styles that ain't even invented yet. He had mad styles.

It might be kind of smooth having a kung fu dog. Especially one that had one of those housecoats with powers in them.

But that other stuff about Coly Jo's moms sleeping to death is kind of freaky. I can't even *picture* that. That kind of thing will make you not want to get too comfortable, that's for sure. If you get to thinking about that too much you won't even want to close your eyes.

You'd rather just think about a dog.

SOMETIMES YOU WAKE UP AFTER BLACK-out and it is so dark you can't even see that treehand in the window. And you can't see that patch hole light or the wall next to your bunk or your own fingers in front of your face either. That kind of blackness is so black you get that floating feeling. I'm floating in that blackness and I'm waiting for my eyes to catch onto some moonlight, but there must be mad clouds blocking the sky tonight.

I have fallen asleep on my lookout shift and my eyes are wide cause I can hear someone in our patch walking with those Indian feet. Those feet sound like whispers.

I can't see him but I can hear his breathing and now it sounds like there are two of them and that breathing sounds like a saw on some wood.

I'm sitting up in the top bunk now, looking for the light, and there is still that breathing. Things start to speed up like the patch air has been cribbed and I can't tell if I am dreaming or if I just caught a room having a thought, cause rooms have thoughts and you can catch your patch having a thought sometimes if you wake up and hear that saw-breath. And why is the reading light off? Coly Jo always sticks it on before he sleeps cause he is afraid of the dark. Coly Jo cries into the back of his elbow sometimes and he likes to watch people sleep and right now I am afraid of the dark and now those Indian feet are shuffling and there is the sound of splash-water like a fishtank has been busted and some of those smooching noises and laughing and more smooching noises and that splash-water smells mad thick and everything feels like a scream when it's trapped in your stomach and my lungwind is seizing up on me and you got to keep your lungwind up if you're clipping hoodies. Damn, that splash-water smells. God, it smells. *Come on, Sura, come on, man . . .*

I find the reading lamp. The light stops that floating feeling and I am still now. Someone's draped a blanket over our window.

Coly Jo is sitting in his bed now and he is crying without sound. It's that kind of not-crying where you can see all of the teeth and inside the mouth hole. His face is crumpled up like a bag. His hands are fire-hands again and they are outstretched in front of him like he is pushing up against something but there ain't nothing to push up against but some air and you can't push up against air.

His arms are wet and his baldy is wet and his face is wet and now I know that that splash-water smell is juvy piss cause there are shitblobs all over his bed and on the floor and those shitblobs look like blackened starfish resting there like they crawled in secret through the window and fell asleep on his bunk.

Coly Jo keeps making that face and his mouth keeps crying but there ain't no sound . . .

After I pick up those shitblobs and throw those sheets away, I help Coly Jo down to the shower and let him use my sanitary bucket cause his got cribbed. He won't even take the soap flakes in his hand. He just stands there with that look on his face and those red crow feet dried up on his belly.

Coly Jo is already starting to turn into a man. He's got some of that Afro hair between his legs and I got a thought that Boo and Hodge might have more Afro hair there, and I also got a thought that having some juvy piss and shitblobs thrown on you could stop that kind of hair from growing for a while.

"Take the soap flakes, man," I say, "take em." But Coly Jo just stands there under the water making that non-crying sound.

I wash him cause he won't. I rub those soap flakes on him so they foam up. When I lift his arm to wash that piss off, that arm just drops to his side like it don't got no bone.

After we are finished I dry him with my towel and walk him back down to our patch and flip his mattress and give him one of my sheets and my Red Troutman's fireproof windbreaker to sleep in.

I sit on the side of Coly Jo's bed until those seizing noises stop in his chest and his lungwind goes smooth.

Sometimes your body will just turn itself off after something like that happens. It knows that the mind can clean itself if it is shut off. I know about that shit cause after I got caught clipping hoodies and that cop busted me in the hamstrings with his blackjack, I felt my body start to turn itself off. By the time I got to the police station I was asleep and dreaming that blue light and they had to snap one of those floor cleaner pills under my nose.

After Coly Jo turns himself off, I crib that blanket and throw it in the hallway. Then I look at that night table Boo makes me rent and I open it up and take my pens out and carry it down to the end of the hall and set it in front of his patch.

The hallway's got that dead sound, like it's listening. It's so quiet that that faucet dripping in the bathroom sounds like a church clock.

Back in the patch I turn the desk light back on and climb up in my bunk. I lay up for the rest of the night. That treehand is huge on our window.

I think about how I busted up that kid who cribbed my hoodies. I think about how I found that can of Sterno and how I wish I had it here at Hamstock sometimes. I think about how I could stick it in my closet under some laundry and then I'd have something for those night creepers. I'd have something for Hodge and Boo Boxfoot.

Before Slider got sent down to St. Chuck's, he told me a story he read about some war soldiers who go into this village and force all the people to give up their dogs and cats so they can make winter coats out of their fur. They need to stay warm cause they are fighting in some snow in the mountains. All of the villagers go and get their dogs and cats and give them to the soldiers.

After the soldiers leave the town this little kid is flying a kite and it gets stuck in a tree just outside the village. When he goes to get his kite he finds all of that pet fur just sitting bloody and dead in a pile with some horseflies on it. And next to that pile is another pile of the skinned pets. They were just left there like that.

Those soldiers didn't need that fur. They didn't even need it.

After Slider told me that story I picked up some rocks and whipped them at a streetlight. I stood there and whipped those rocks for a long time. I whipped those rocks until I busted that streetlight, too.

I don't understand that story about those soldiers. I don't understand none of it.

MISTER TULLY'S RASPBERRY SPOT LOOKS like a map on his face. He is holding my anklebones, going, "Bust a gut, Sura! Bust a gut!"

The parking lot is cold and hard on my back, but I am quick and my stomach is strong. Every time I bust a situp I can see Mister Tully's long, white war jaw and that purple map on his face.

The air is cold and you can see your breath smoking. All of that juvy breath is rising off the parking lot.

Gut drill lasts for twenty minutes every morning. It's the first activity after the aurora horn. That six-thirty horn sounds like a fire alarm and if you ain't out in front of your patch hole by the time it's done blowing Mister Rose will carp you with the quickness.

It's strange how juvies look standing outside of their patch holes after the aurora horn blows. Usually they all look like a bunch of juvies with cribbing and chucking and buffaloing on their minds. But after the aurora horn blows they just stand there rubbing their faces and yawning and leaning on the wall like the night has put those thoughts in a box for a few minutes. That's the only time they look like some regular kids.

At gut drill all you do is pushups and situps. Sometimes Mister Tully will run you in place, too, but that's only when you're late, and if that happens he'll run you until your lungwind seizes up and you can't lift your knees.

After situps you get a minute break. Most juvies lie on their backs like they're trying to crib part of that dream they were dreaming before the aurora horn. Sometimes I'll do that, too, especially when I dream about those Choate Street Honeys.

Coly Jo is standing in front of the fence with his hand hanging over his belly. He's looking out over those bean fields. He's done that between every set now and he's lucky Mister Tully ain't carped him yet. There was a frost last night and it looks like those fields are covered with cake mix.

Slider wrote me a letter after my first week and told me about an abandoned tractor shed that's three miles north of Hamstock. It's right next to this pond that's got an old ride sticking out of the shallow end. Slider's patch mate—this kid they called Hurricane—escaped and hid out there for three days until he jumped a freight train. Two months later he sent Slider a map to that shed. A week after he sent that map he was shot in the head in front of a movie theater. Hurricane was a gangbanger who went back to gangbanging.

When I get out of here, the last thing I'm going to do is go back to clipping hoodies. That'd be like eating some bad meat and getting sick and then going back to that same hunk of meat just cause you're hungry.

When I get out of here I might try slinging some craps or running digits for a while, but I ain't going back to clipping hoodies, that's for damn sure.

Hurricane was the only juvy to ever make a clean bust from Hamstock. Slider would've done it, too, but he got transferred to St. Chuck's before he had the chance.

I got that map taped inside my history book now. Sometimes I'll sit in study box and just memorize that map and picture myself running those three miles to that shed . . .

Mister Tully blows on his whistle and Coly Jo jogs away from the fence all pigeon-toed and slumping and the rest of us return to our spots.

Then Mister Tully blows on his whistle again and we are busting pushups.

Demetrius Gord always comes into the shower room sporting a sex pole. He can't even wear his towel cause that sex pole sticks straight out into the air like a treehand.

If you wake up with a sex pole it usually goes away after you bust that morning piss. But Demetrius Gord's always got one. And he'll stand there and show it to you, too, like it's something he won at the carnival. It's probably the biggest sex pole you'll ever see.

As long as he stays under his shower head and keeps it to himself I could care less if he puts hotsauce on it.

Some juvies got those skin flaps on the end of their dicks. It makes them look like some elephant trunks. Coly Jo's got one like that. Mines is clipped in just the right place, though. I'm glad I don't got no skin flap. I'll bet you just get stuff all up in it all the time. Once I saw Coly Jo cleaning his with a Q-tip.

When you shower in Spalding you got to be fast. And you got to keep your sanitary bucket right at your feet or else a juvy will crib it while you're flushing some soap flakes out of your eyes.

I'll tell you, a black juvy with white soap flakes all over his body is just about the most bugged-out thing you'll see at Hamstock. It looks like his skin got burned off in a fire. Slider warned me about that.

I know when I got soap flakes all over my body it just makes me look shinier.

One time I used so much soap that I got some all up in my dick hole and that made it mad burn when I pissed. So I went right over to Nurse Rushing's office and had her take a look at it and just about busted a sex pole when she started touching me with those smooth hands.

The funny thing is that she knew that I got some soap flakes all up in my dick hole. She told me to come back in three days if it didn't stop burning. Part of old Sura wanted to go back there for another examination, but that burning stopped. So now I'm mad careful when I'm soaping up with those flakes.

The towels they give you at Hamstock are about as thin as Kleenex. Mister Rose hands them to you on your way back to your patch.

When I leave the shower Mister Rose asks me where Coly Jo is and I tell him that he's down at our patch doing some homework.

"That boy better start sanitizing himself," Mister Rose says. I think about how Coly Jo ain't showered since I washed those shitblobs off him.

"Yes sir, Mister Rose," I say.

"You tell him I better see him in here after slate docket."

"Yes sir, Mister Rose."

"I'll take his dirty ass outside tomorrow morning and hose him down at gut drill."

"Yes sir, Mister Rose," I say again.

"Dirty-ass juvies," Mister Rose says. And he says it to me all mean and hard with those wide-spread shark eyes, like *I'm* the dirtiest juvy in Spalding. Then he hands me a towel and I walk back to my patch.

COLY JO IS FILLING HIS PLATE WITH BREAKfast hash. His hands are slow and his feet are slow and his mouth hangs funny like he's trying to hide some gum.

At the hash line I tell him about what Mister Rose said, and I say it quiet cause a juvy will latch on to that information and by the time you get to your table the whole hash house will know. And they'll thump on shit with their spoons, too, just to let you know that they know. But Coly Jo don't seem interested in what I'm saying. He ain't even looking at me.

When he sits down I say it again, but his eyes just stare off glazed and yellow like some floor cleaner. When he chews his food his mouth is slow. And when he drinks his milk his hand is slow.

He's got that kind of quiet you get sometimes that makes everyone around you quiet. They'll watch you and follow you with their eyes and wait for you to say something, but you just stare at your hand or at the wall or at some cracks in the ceiling. That silence comes from the eyes and the parts of the face around the eyes. It comes from your lungwind and your heartbeats. It makes you still. That kind of silence says more than Mister Rose's big dictionary words say, but you don't know what it means. It makes you feel like you got a fist all clenched up inside your stomach.

I went silent like that after I got caught clipping hoodies. Mazzy walked out of that courtroom with that look on her face and later in the ride she started crying and telling me about Hamstock Boys Center and how I got six months. I was mad silent for about three days.

When Coly Jo finishes his plate he stares down at his lap. I look over at Boo and Hodge's table and they are waving at me and smiling with those milk smears on their mouths. I just eat my food and try to not-think about that splash-water. *Don't look back at their table,* I tell myself. *Don't do it, Sura.*

It's mad hard to keep your eyes off of something like that, though. If a tiger was in the middle of the street you wouldn't just look at the sidewalk; you'd look right at that tiger so you'd know where he was walking.

"Go get some seconds, man," I tell Coly Jo. I want him to get thirds and fourths, too. I think that that hash house food might put a grub smile back on his face. "Go on, Coly Jo," I say.

But he just sits there staring down at his lap. His baldy catches that hash house light like a bowling ball. He ain't getting up. The way he keeps looking down at his lap makes it seem like he ain't never going to take seconds again.

When he finally looks up at me, those sick eyes are burning yellow.

I am sitting in Miss Denton's slate docket and she is talking about some Pilgrims and how they came over on a boat and how so many of them got sick and died from fevers.

After a while, you can't listen to Miss Denton no more. She teaches all of your subjects, and after the first two her voice starts to go mad flat.

I decide to pull out *Sura's Smooth Seven,* some important general rules I got about the Honeys. It's the kind of thing that'll take your mind off of shit, like all of that waving Boo and Hodge was doing at the hash house. I'm glad I don't got slate docket with them. I heard how Hodge messed up on his skills test just so he could stay in the lower slate docket with Boo.

I keep *Sura's Smooth Seven* folded up in my reading book so it don't get wrinkled.

Sura's Smooth Seven

1. If a Honey is talking to her friends and you want her attention, give your wristbands a couple of good tugs and start lighting matches. Light them one at a time and hold them in front of you so they flame up nice and bright. Lighting a match will make them all look at you. Just make sure to throw some mad sexy eyes at the one you're smooth on. If that Honey don't come right over,

do it again two minutes later. Wood matches are best cause they burn slower. Whatever you do, man, don't burn those fingers.

2. When roller skating with a Honey, lay that hand flat on the small of her back and guide her. If that back starts to feel warm like it's cooking, that means she's smooth on you. Then you take her over to the corner and show her the lining of your Red Troutman's fireproof windbreaker. If she touches it, it means that she's good to go. You can bet your favorite hoody that you'll get those phone digits and a mouth kiss.

3. If you're at the bowling alley and one of the Honey Buns (Heather Fogg or Lacy Meyerhoff) is hanging out, wait for her to pick out a ball, tape a square on your ear, walk over to her, and pull out a top-shelf hoody (a Benzo or a Jag). Stick the hoody on her arm or her shoulder. If she takes it and throws some eyes at you, introduce yourself and invite her over to your lane and move to the last part of rule number two (but don't unsnap your windbreaker too fast—do it smooth like Slider showed you). If she pushes the hoody away, break north with the quickness. Don't stand around so Old Man Kegley at the shoe counter has a chance to page security. Break north, man.

4. For older Honeys: Sport a pair of shorts under your jeans so you'll look thicker. Talk about stuff that a teacher might talk about. Throw some poetry at her (get from Slider; he keeps the good stuff in his hoody bag). Offer her clove squares. Use a curse word every three or four sentences.

5. For younger Honeys: First, find out if she's got an older brother. Don't mess with little sisters, man. If she is sporting a tank top, throw a quarter over her head so she's got to lift her arms to catch it. If she's got underarm smears, then she's good to go. If not, introduce her to Bunky over on Fourth Street. He's only eleven and he's got a pretty smooth dead frog collection.

6. If you're at a movie with her, sit in the front row so she's got to look up. When that neck starts to get sore, offer a quick rub, just above the shoulders. If she says okay, put that smooth Sura hand on the back of her neck and rub left to right and wait till it starts cooking (you know what to do next, Sura). If she says no, tell her you're going to go buy some popcorn and call Turner and Huxley to see if they're playing spades. If they are, break north, man.

7. If she's got long hair, when she ain't looking, throw a paper clip so it sticks. Then walk up to her and pull it out (but be smooth, man). If that

Honey throws some eyes at you, send a prop her way. Maybe something like: "I noticed the sun on your hair," or "What shampoo do you use?" If the paper clip gets tangled and you can't get it out, offer her a stick of gum and leave it alone.

Whenever I get bored at slate docket, I just pull out *Sura's Smooth Seven*. You can never get bored with the Honeys.

Sometimes in the middle of one of those stories about Pilgrims or Honest Abe or whatever else Miss Denton's bumping at the gums about, you can get to clock-watching too much, and whenever you clock-watch like that, time slows down with the quickness. And it's like Hamstock *knows* you're clock-watching, too—like someone is inside the wall holding back that second hand with some string.

If you fall asleep in slate docket, Miss Denton will carp you *and* tell Dean Petty, and he'll paddle your ass with the quickness. So shit like *Sura's Smooth Seven* and Hurricane's bust-out map comes in mad handy. I've added three rules since I've been at Hamstock. It used to be called *Sura's Famous Four*.

It wouldn't be so bad if Miss Denton was something to look at, but she's about seventy years old. You could be locked up at Hamstock for fifty years and that body of hers wouldn't ever start to look better. She's built like a Christmas tree, and if she didn't have those mad pointy bosoms, you would think she was a man. I wouldn't want to chuck with her, either; she's got those blue muscle-veins all over her forearms.

You hear about how they teach all the Hamstock staff karate and judo and shit, just in case a juvy gets out of hand and tries to start a chuck. I ain't never seen it happen, though, not even with that skinny guy who sacks the garbage at the hash house. They call him Butterhead cause he always sports this shower cap on his Afro and underneath that shower cap his hair is full of activator juice. Butterhead ain't no bigger than me and he walks with a limp and he'll fall down sometimes and have trouble getting up, but you'll never catch a juvy snapping on him, not even Boo or Hodge.

There's something about adults that always makes you feel like a kid. Even those skinny weaklings who sport shower caps and fall down all the time. It's like they all know karate or judo or something.

Chuckie Steptoe is waiting for me at the edge of the rabbit line. You can't miss Chuckie Steptoe cause he sports these glasses with shag-carpeted frames. You almost get that chocolate milk belly up every time you see him. What's funny is that they're medicine glasses. You can tell by looking through them when he sets them down in slate docket. They go all thick and wavy. It's hard to believe that a kid's moms would get him some shag-carpeted medicine glasses.

So Chuckie Steptoe is waiting for me with those bugged-out glasses on and he tells me he wants to race me. For second hash I filled up pretty good on some of those pizza pockets. I feel mad thick in the middle. And

Chuckie Steptoe looks all shiny and quick with his walk like he's been busting some wind sprints to warm up. Chuckie Steptoe's got those froglegs, too.

Down at the other side of the rabbit line there are about ten juvies changing hands like they got tenths on the race. Even though they are eleven or twelve seconds away you can see those smiles on their faces like they think old Sura is going to finally get knocked off.

My blood starts mad cooking. It's hard to get those happy feet up when you're all thick in the middle with some pizza pockets. But I take a second and stretch those leg muscles and step to that scuff mark. Chuckie Steptoe takes those glasses off and holds them in his hand and gets all low to the ground like he's going to bust a fart or something and then a juvy at the other end of the line raises his hand and in the back of my mind I picture that cop with his blackjack and me with my hoody bag mad flying off my side and then that hand goes down and then there's that whistle and I am off with eleven seconds of the quickness . . .

I walk back to Spalding alone. When I look back Chuckie Steptoe is sitting down at the finish line with that head of his propped up at the sky. He's putting those glasses back on and mad shaking his head, just like all the other rabbits.

After slate docket I walk back to Spalding. When I come off the stairs I can see Mister Rose down by the showers. He's leaning up against the wall swinging a towel, looking all bored like he's waiting for a bus. Other juvies are coming off the stairs and dropping their books in their patches.

I walk back downstairs and look for Coly Jo. Now that he's got that flat baldy you can spot him from a long ways off.

He ain't in study box and he ain't in the basement and he ain't outside walking back from slate docket with the other juvies either, so I walk back into Spalding.

When I come off the stairs again, Mister Rose just shakes his head all slow and mean, like it's *my* fault that Coly Jo didn't show up to sanitize himself. Then he throws that towel over his shoulder and walks away from the shower.

That night table is back. It is crooked and wobbly like someone's thrown it up against the wall. And what makes it worse is that it's upside down.

Walking into your patch and seeing something like that is just about the worst thing that can happen to you cause you know Boo is going to be waiting for you at juvy pound with his big white palm hungry for that six tenths. And you know he'll make sure to get in line before you, too, so he can collect his bone-and-twenty and hang out by the fire doors and wait for you.

Dear Slider,

What's up, man, how's St. Chuck's? You running that joint yet? They still serving that nasty food? How much time you got left?

Hamstock is still Hamstock, nothing but chucking and ducking. We had a lice check but I was clean. I wouldn't let them touch my hair noways even if I had maggots in it. They would have to strap me down with some ropes, I'll tell you that.

Things were pretty smooth for a minute but shit is getting kind of hectic lately. I know I only got four months left but this shit is starting to get to me. This juvy life ain't the life of Riley, that's for sure.

Hodge buffaloed Petey Sessoms the other day. Juvies just stood around and watched too. My patch mate is getting mixed up in some heavy stuff. He don't go for none of this shit but he ain't Petey Sessoms. He ain't even half of Petey Sessoms. He's just got that mad thick pride.

Hodge and Boo are going to start calling me out. I can feel it. Man, I think something bad is about to go down.

The Hurricane map is heavy on my head and my lungwind is up. I've been busting it at gut drill. I keep picturing that pond in my mind like you told me.

My hoody bag is hidden back home behind the reservoir. I got a few hundred bones in it. After I get out of here I'm breaking north. Let me know your plans.

STAY UP, MAN . . .

Sura

WHEN THE AURORA HORN BLOWS YOU fall out in front of your patch hole and listen to that roar. It'll clean that dream out of your mind with the quickness.

Usually Mister Rose is right there in the hallway, hitting the junk can with his broom handle. Sometimes he hits it so hard you'd think he was setting off firecrackers. If you ain't out in the hall by the time he walks by, he'll bust right through your patch hole and stick you with that broom handle. Today he ain't there, though. It's just a bunch of juvies bobbing off the wall and looking around and waiting for that aurora horn to die.

I look back into my patch and I see that Coly Jo ain't even in there, and the next thing you know, Mister Rose is coming around the stairwell with a face like he is toting some heavy bags.

"Go on and get ready for gut drill!" he shouts at us through his teeth.

Right after that, Coly Jo appears at the end of Mister Rose's arm. Mister Rose is pulling him by his belt. Coly Jo's lungwind is all seized up and his shirt is off and his fat belly is shiny and those jeans are so wet they look like they've been painted.

Some juvies are still watching and then Mister Rose shouts at them again. "Go on, goddamnit!" he says. "Go on!" Then he throws Coly Jo through the patch hole.

Coly Jo is fighting for that patch air like one of those little kids who gets scared underwater at the public pool. His mouth is all seized up by his gums.

"I'll teach you somethin about sanitizin!" Mister Rose says to him in that mean voice. Those eyes of his are mean, too. I wouldn't play spades against him if you paid me. I couldn't even concentrate, looking at those nasty shark eyes. Coly Jo's back just keeps lifting up with those gasps.

At gut drill we are busting some pushups when Mister Rose comes walking out to the parking lot. He's got Coly Jo by the neck. Coly Jo is sporting a towel and carrying my sanitary bucket. With that white towel on he looks blacker than you've ever seen him.

Mister Rose is carrying a fire extinguisher in his other hand. The way he is pushing Coly Jo by the neck you'd think he is going to shoot him like they do in a war.

Mister Tully blows his whistle and we all stop busting pushups and stand up. Mister Rose pushes Coly Jo up against the fence and snatches that towel. Coly Jo's eyes are wet and his dick has shriveled up like a little wrinkled doll part. Then Mister Rose pushes him up against this part of the fence that's behind this little storage shed. The last thing Mister Rose wants is Deacon Bob Fly or Miss Denton or Nurse Rushing walking by, someone who might help you. The last thing he wants is one of those cars on the highway slowing down to watch.

You can't even see Coly Jo no more. All you can see is Mister Rose and Coly Jo's breath smoking out of the side of that shed.

Then Mister Rose reaches into my sanitary bucket and starts throwing soap flakes at Coly Jo and he is throwing them like he is throwing a ball, like he is trying to make those soap flakes sting.

Mister Rose tells Coly Jo to raise his arms and then he disappears behind the shed for a second and you just know he's mushing those soap flakes into Coly Jo's pits and smearing them on his face and over his baldy. Then Mister Rose appears again, raises up that fire extinguisher, and shoots that hard water all over Coly Jo. Then Mister Rose tells him to turn around and starts spraying him again, and you just know he's shooting that fire water at his ass and all up in his crack.

Some rides are passing by on the highway, but they don't slow down at all. They just keep zooming by like Hamstock ain't even there.

I look around me and there ain't one juvy laughing. Not even Boo and Hodge. They're just standing around with those non-looks on their faces and that smoky breath leaking out of their mouths.

When Mister Rose is finished, he throws the towel at Coly Jo and hands him my sanitary bucket. When Coly Jo comes out from behind that shed his face just looks like deadness. Then Mister Rose lifts that extinguisher, grabs Coly Jo by his neck, and pushes him back toward Spalding.

After they leave, Mister Tully blows his whistle and we are back on the ground. We are on our backs this time busting situps. Just like that, like nothing happened at all.

That ground is cold and hard. It's harder than you've ever felt it before. Like the night did something to it, like it stuck a bunch of rocks in it. You wouldn't want to feel it. Not for a second. It ain't even worth talking about.

DEACON BOB FLY IS USING THUMB PUPPETS. He's got one on each hand. They got those plastic kewpie-doll faces with some bugged-out eyes and painted-on hair. He is using strange voices and attaching those voices to the puppets, but I can't understand what he is saying cause in my mind I can't stop snapping on the way those puppets look.

You just *know* that the people in the factory who put those puppets together don't give a damn about them. You can just tell. They probably just stick their hands into a box of puppet parts and force those parts together. They probably don't even *look* at them while they're doing it, either. They probably just smoke squares or flip digits or something.

Even with those bugged-out eyes those thumb puppets look like deadness. They got those non-looks on their faces.

Deacon Bob Fly has asked me to put the thumb puppets on and pretend like they're my moms and pops. Damn, that's some stupid shit.

First of all, you can't just *do* that. You can't just stick puppets on your thumbs and act out stuff like that. At least I can't. That kind of shit ain't for Sura, that's for sure.

You might catch some *little kid* playing like that. You sometimes see those finger puppets that you can cut out of the back of a cereal box. You've seen little kids with those, and how they'll be playing with them in the front of a grocery cart or some place. It can even be kind of smooth, too, if the kid is singing a song with them or disguising his voice. You could handle that. You could even *enjoy* that.

But if I was behind one of those fake mirrors and I was watching a kid *my age* playing with thumb puppets, I would think he might have a little gasoline on the brain.

Second of all, Deacon Bob Fly wants me to pretend like they're my moms and pops, and they don't even look like they're old enough to make a baby. They're so bugged-out-looking that they don't even look like they got sex parts.

Besides, I wouldn't know my pops from a tube of toothpaste. It would be like putting those puppets on your thumbs and pretending like one of them is your moms and the other one is the man on the moon.

I used to try and imagine what my pops was like. I used to picture some guy with slick hair and a briefcase. For some reason, that's all I would see—his hair and that briefcase. I would try to picture other parts of him, too, like an arm or a nose, but every time I would try that, some mad freaky stuff would start happening. For instance, I would start out picturing that briefcase, and then I'd move up to his arm cause that's what the briefcase is attached to, but then the arm that would show up in my mind would be a *dog's* arm. And it would be all hairy and skinny and there would be some horseflies on it. That kind of shit would happen all the time like that, so I had to stop.

"Go on, Sura," Deacon Bob Fly says. "Take the puppets."

I take those puppets and I look at them in my hands. I look at that painted-on hair and those bugged-out eyes.

"Good, Sura," Deacon Bob Fly says. "There you go."

And then my head gets mad heavy for some reason and my hands are fire-hands and my lungwind starts seizing up and there is one of those moments that you can't really talk about. It's one of those times when you feel like something is cooking in your blood. You just close your eyes and wait for that cooking to stop.

I think it's cause of this memory I get sometimes:

Someone is hitting Mazzy in the face with a phonebook. She's crying and pushing out with her hands. But he's too strong. The skinny guy with the beard is too strong and he keeps busting her. And he's calling her mad names. But those names don't really sound like words, they sound more like those garbage truck screams. The skinny guy rips out a phonebook page and balls it up and stuffs it in her mouth. He makes her eat it. And her face is wet and she can't really chew it cause her mouth won't work. And the skinny guy is using both hands to try and *make* it work.

I am little. I'm so small it's like I ain't even there. The parts inside me are all there, like my lungs and my heart, but everything else—my hands and my arms and my legs—everything else feels like it's disappearing. And I'm moving my mouth but I don't even got no voice yet.

He ain't my pops cause he don't got one of those dog

arms, but I don't really know for sure. All I know is that that skinny guy stops making all of that noise, and then he leaves. When he leaves, those garbage truck screams stop and it feels like he disappears, and his disappearing makes it feel like my heart and my lungs are disappearing with everything else, like the other side of the front door ain't nothing but blackness and I am part of that blackness . . .

"Sura . . . ?" Deacon Bob Fly says. "You okay?" Deacon Bob Fly has made my face wet again. Damn, I hate that big yellow head of his.

"Fuck you," I say. Then I pull the heads off those dumbass thumb puppets.

He just stares at me for a second. Then he goes, "I want to help you, son."

But then I go "Fuck you" again.

Then he is writing all of this chicken scratch down on his notebook. Nothing but chicken scratch.

At the juvy pound line we are all facing the wall. You're always on your best behavior at the juvy pound line cause Mister Rose will carp you with the quickness, just so he can tell that woman handing out your bone-and-twenty to cut away some tenths.

Once, Mister Rose carped this juvy for busting a fart and cut away four tenths. Usually all the other juvies would start laughing at something like that, but not in the juvy pound line. It was one of those farts that sounds like someone blowing on a horn. You can't help that shit, though, especially when that hash house food starts shifting around inside you. You're liable to bust a fart at any time. But Mister Rose wouldn't go for it. That kid was mad pissed off too, cause he needed his whole juvy pound so he could buy some comics.

If I ever got to bust a fart I'll mad squeeze it in unless I'm in my patch. You got to learn how to shift those toilet muscles around inside you. The body can learn that kind of shit. You can't afford to get carped for busting a fart.

So we are standing in line and facing the wall and out of the side of my eye I can see Boo getting his juvy pound and stepping off to the fire doors. Then Hodge gets his and steps off. And then two other juvies get theirs, and then it's my turn.

I ain't been carped this week, so the woman pushes me my full bone-and-twenty through the little opening in the glass and tells me to step off.

When I reach the fire doors, Boo is leaning up against them all slumping and lazy like there ain't no bone in his back.

He sticks his hand out like he always does, expecting his six tenths. I can see Hodge at the end of the hall, turning left and right with those lookout eyes.

I stare at that hand for a long time and then I move that stare up and look at Boo's harelip and shake my head. I shake it about four times.

"You must be crazy, Sura," Boo says.

I don't answer him. I just try to step off down the hall, but Boo pushes that big fist of his into my chest. And he starts pushing it hard, too, so it feels like a brick.

Now his other hand has sneaked around my back and he is pulling me into his fist.

"I'll bust a hole in your chest, Sura," he says, all quiet.

Boo's got that man-strength, and that brick fist feels like it's going to blast through me. For a second I think I'm going to fall down cause that pain is sharp now, like that brick fist's got a spike on the end of it.

So I fling my arm out and when I do that the fire door flies open and the alarm goes off. Boo jumps back so quick you'd think he got stuck with a fish hook. That fire alarm is mad loud, and it don't sound nothing like the aurora horn. It sounds like a bunch of atomic bombs busting or something. Boo breaks north with the quickness.

There ain't nothing like watching juvies scrambling around Spalding when the fire alarm goes off. It's like watching a bunch of turkeys busting it to escape that Thanksgiving hunter. You can't even name all the directions those juvies are running in.

It's so much fun you'd think juvies would spend less time playing floor hockey and more time messing with those fire doors.

Dean Petty's paddle feels like a bunch of beestings when it busts you in the ass. It *is* two feet long and it *does* got air holes and he *does* hang it above his desk. It's the first thing you see when you walk into his office.

Dean Petty is a big white man and when he walks across the room he takes those long, slow strides like he is walking in a dream.

He is over at this blackboard. He takes a piece of chalk in his hand and writes "FIRE DOORS" in big capital letters, so big that they cover the entire blackboard.

It's kind of funny how Dean Petty don't even speak. He won't even call out your name to come into his office. He just comes into the hall and points at you the way you point at a dog when it's caught shitting in the house.

And when you're in his office he points you over to his big iron desk and then he lets the blinds down and closes the door and when that door closes you feel like you got a bunch of glass in your stomach.

After that he folds you up so your body hangs all over his desk. And then he spreads your legs wide and pulls your drawers down and grabs that paddle with that long reach. And then he takes his suit coat off and rolls up those sleeves so you can see those muscle parts in his forearms.

You just try to take your mind off it by looking at those papers spread out on that iron desk, or by listening for that Hamstock wall clock clipping time, or by looking at that picture frame with that Honey in it who looks like she might be your age and she's got some smooth long blond hair and a gold butterfly pin on her sweater and that kind of smile where her mouth is barely open so you can just see a little bit of teeth like she just finished some gum and those blue eyes are looking back at you and they're the kind of blue eyes that you could just stare at until you go all dry in the mouth . . .

Then Dean Petty tells you to lift your head up and when you do you realize he's got you set up so that you can look right at that blackboard when he's swatting you.

So you wait and you keep reading those big white letters and the thoughts of that Honey in the picture frame get cleaned out of your head with the quickness and you actually start picturing those fire doors in your mind and then comes that swooshing sound like some wind in a busted window, and then *wop . . . wop . . . wop . . . wop . . .* with those long wind-up pauses in between.

After the fourth swat your ass and your waist and the backs of your legs go numb and it don't hurt as much. But those first four are kind of what I always thought lightning might feel like. That pain shoots clear through you. And all you hear is your own non-voice screaming through all of that glass in your stomach cause Dean Petty won't say a word. He's just there to swat you, like that's the only reason he's been put on the earth.

When he's finished he points you over to the blackboard and makes you clean those words right off with a wet rag. And you're so bugged-out that your hands are fire-hands. And your mouth might be twitching, too.

And while you're cleaning that blackboard Dean Petty is just shuffling through some of those papers on his desk, and you start to feel like *you* are one of those papers that he's shuffling through, like he could just ball you up and throw you in his junk can and not think twice about it.

When you're finished cleaning the blackboard you can leave. You got to take your time walking cause everything gets mad wobbly. That glass in your stomach is mad crashing around.

And for a moment you look back at Dean Petty. For some reason you think he might nod at you or shake his head or something. But all he does is stick that paddle back on the wall.

Dean Petty won't even say good-bye. He just puts that suit coat back on, pulls the blinds up, and points you out the door.

At the hash house Coly Jo and I are standing in line for some grub. The hash house guards make you stand in single file, face-to-back-of-the-head, and if you goof in that line they'll carp you and take that grub away and make you wash some dishes.

We got our trays in our hands and that line is long with juvies. It gets long like that when Butterhead and those hash house Honeys roll out the grub wagon.

Coly Jo is standing in front of me and his tray is hanging at his side. He ain't grubbed in mad days.

Behind me I can hear Boo and Hodge and some other juvies talking. You can't tell whose voice is whose cause they're busting whispers. It's kind of like when you are in that YMCA room and you can hear a good game of spades being played in the room next to yours. You don't know who's talking and you can't imagine faces with those voices, but you can picture those cards all fanned out and some hands holding them and maybe some rings on those hands.

"Look at that boy, Ock."

"Look at him."

"He can't even hold that tray."

"Can't even hold it, Ock."

"That's a shame, ain't it, Ock."

"A *shame*."

"Holdin it like a *bitch* like that."

"A damn shame, Ock."

A hash house guard walks by and those juvies behind me stop talking. When he has passed with those big neck muscles all up on his shoulders they start up again busting those whispers.

"Yo, Ock, we gonna get him?"

"Yeah, Ock, we gonna get him."

"Yeah?"

"Yeah, Ock."

"Yo, Ock, we gonna take those nuts?"

"Yeah, Ock, we gonna take those nuts."

"For real?"

"For real, Ock."

"Yo, Ock, we gonna *sell* those nuts?"

"Yeah, Ock, we gonna sell those nuts."

"Who we gonna sell em to, Ock?"

"Who we gonna sell em to?"

"Yeah, Ock, who's the lucky buyer?"

"The lucky buyer is his *moms*, Ock."

"His *moms?*"

"Yeah, Ock."

"For real?"

"The woman who *made* him?"

"What's *she* gonna do with em, Ock?"

"What's *she* gonna do with em?"

"Tell me, Ock."

"What's she gonna *do*?"

"Ock, tell me, Ock."

"She's gonna stuff them nuts in her *mouth,* Ock."

"Then what, Ock?"

"*Then* what?"

"Tell me, Ock, tell me."

"What else, Ock? She's gonna *chew.*"

I look down and Coly Jo's hand is a fire-hand again. That tray is vibrating so much it looks electric.

The thing about "Ock" is that you never know who he is. Sometimes you think "Ock" could be one juvy, and sometimes you think "Ock" could be eleven juvies. It's one of those non-words that some of the juvies throw around. It's kind of like the way you say "man" sometimes. You wish you could just look up the word "Ock" in Mister Rose's book and see a picture next to it.

I knew this kid around my way they called "Mastiff" and I looked up that word and saw a picture of this big Saint Bernard dog next to it. They'll sometimes throw a picture in the word book like that. But you just *know* Ock is one of those non-words.

Those juvies keep whispering behind me. It seems like more have joined in. I just keep looking at that tray. I mad hope that Coly Jo don't drop it.

When your moms visits you they stick you in a room with a day guard and sit you at a hash table with two chairs and some cups of water. That day guard just sits in a chair by the door and flips through some stuff on his clipboard and looks over at you once in a while.

This is Mazzy's second time visiting me. The first time we just sat there at that table and stared at each other like we had new parts on our faces. At one point she reached over and cleaned my chin with some mouth spit. Her eyes were all glazed and sad-looking. When I started looking down at my knees I thought she was going to give me one of those smooth Mazzy hugs where she pulls you in so tight you get that smoky feeling in your head, but she didn't.

When the guard called her away and told her visiting time was over, she cried into her fishing hat and mad squeezed my hand. Then she gave me that letter with the picture of Flintlock's house in it. She pulled it out of her fishing hat like she thought she had to hide it.

It's pretty smooth how Mazzy will sport a fishing hat like that. She don't know the first thing about fishing, but she'll sport that hat and flip the bill up so you can see those big Mazzy eyes.

She's brought me another letter. She don't hide it in her hat this time; she just hands it to me. Deacon Bob Fly's the one who thought it would be a good idea if we exchanged some letters. He said how it would make it easier to say things. I ain't written to her yet, though. I guess I just don't know what to say. It ain't easy to think of what to say to your moms when you've messed up real bad. Those thoughts just don't turn into words too smooth. It's like trying to catch some flying feathers when a fan is blowing in a room.

Mazzy pushes that letter toward me and smiles. I picture Mazzy writing me that letter. I picture her sitting at the kitchen table in Flintlock's little house with some paper and a pen. She's got that smooth cursive writing, too. I like the way she makes J's.

I take the letter in my hand and look at all of the different colors on the envelope. There are about twelve colors on that envelope. I picture Mazzy buying that envelope at the pharmacy on Choate Street and telling the old Honey at the cash register how she's buying it for me, how she's busting a letter for her Sura.

I even picture her crumpling up some paper and throwing it in the junk can cause maybe she found some spelling mistakes, or maybe those thoughts didn't come out like she wanted. That's pretty smooth, if you think about it.

So we're sitting in the visitors' room and that day guard is reading his clipboard with his elbows on his knees, and Mazzy is across from me with that fishing hat on. She just watches me and I watch her.

You got to wonder how her dancing is going. You got to wonder if Flintlock is taking her out to the movies and if he's told her all the stories about those tattoos on his arms. You got to wonder if he plays tetherball with her in front of his house, if he stuck a ball back on the string yet. You got mad questions all stopped up inside of you; *mad* questions.

But for some reason, we just sit there like that again. We just sit there and watch each other and watch that day guard watching us. Mazzy is squeezing my hand again. *Mad* squeezing it.

After my visit with Mazzy I am coming around the infirmary when I see someone digging in the ground in back of the dead tree.

From the infirmary it looks like it could be a dog. But when I focus with those big Sura eyes I can see that flat baldy and I know it is Coly Jo.

Coly Jo is digging up the ground with his hands, and when the hole is deep enough so that his hands are disappearing, he reaches into his pocket and pulls out something wrapped in a nose rag. He makes sure those folds are tight and then he looks left and right like he's making sure no one else is around. Slider calls that "billing a spot."

So Coly Jo is billing his spot and then he takes whatever is wrapped in that nose rag and shoves it into the ground. Then he starts scooping the dirt back into the ground.

I don't think I've ever seen Coly Jo bust it so hard at something. I've seen how he can throw down some of that hash house food, and I've even seen him bust through some pushups when he wants to. But this is different. That baldy of his is shining like some wet fudge. He pats the dirt down so it's flat.

You've seen how a dog will bury a bone. You've seen *that* a thousand times. But you ain't never seen a *kid* bury nothing before. Not even hoodies.

SOMEONE STUCK DEMETRIUS GORD IN the shower room. They stuck him with a pencil and broke it off in his side. All you could hear was that double-screaming bouncing off the walls of the shower room. Then there was some scrambling in the hall and the sound juvies make when they're busting it to get through their patch holes and then you could hear that double-screaming again. It was all high-pitched like a boogymonster scream.

Demetrius Gord had to be carried off on a body plate and his side was mad bleeding and one of those guys with the white coats was trying to stop it up with some hospital rags.

That's what will happen if you sanitize yourself alone like that. Ever since juvies found out about Demetrius Gord coming into the shower room sporting those sex poles, juvies got to talking in the hash house and calling him a homo and shit. Like I said, I could care less how his blood cooks up in the shower room. As long as he keeps that sex pole of his to himself, things are smooth with me. But juvies are funny like that. You hear them mad choking off after blackout, and you know they all got those sex poles up, but when they see some swollen sex parts on *another* juvy they act all bugged-out and start creeping up behind you with pencils and shit. Like they ain't *never* busted a sex pole before.

So we are locked up in front of our patches and Mister Rose is telling us how he's going to throw the A-train on us if the juvy who stuck Demetrius Gord in the side with that pencil don't step forward. The A-train means that he'll make us run stair laps all night and into the morning until the aurora horn blows.

It's only happened in Spalding one other time. Someone cribbed the clock out of study box. After about the fortieth lap, juvies were mad falling out and crying for their moms and stuff. I caught about four cramps and my toilet muscles seized up on me and I couldn't bust a shit for about three days.

No one's stepped forward for twenty minutes now and Mister Rose has already had us in pushup position four times. And we had to go halfway down two of those times. Everyone is sweaty and the hallway smells mad thick.

Juvies are cursing at each other with their eyes. Thinking about that A-train is like being tied to a stake with some newspapers at your feet and watching someone with a torch walking slowly toward you. You can barely see him in that wavy distance, but that torch is mad blazing and you can almost *feel* that fire licking those anklebones.

Out of the side of my eye I can see Coly Jo and how

that sweat has settled like some rain in the dented parts of his baldy. Mister Rose yells at us to get down again, this time three-quarters. Juvies just drop down on those wobbly arms. You can barely make it thirty seconds at three-quarters.

So you start shaking and groaning and that fist is mad clenched up in your stomach and all of a sudden Mister Rose is mad busting it toward your patch yelling, "Coly Jo, get your ass out here! Coly Jo!" and when you look up you can see why: Coly Jo never dropped down to do his three-quarters. In fact, he ain't even standing next to you. Before you can get up, Coly Jo is busting it out of your patch toward Mister Rose and he's got that night table mad raised over his head. They look like some wild dogs busting it toward each other like that.

Everything goes silent for a second and all you can hear is Mister Rose's Doctor J's and Coly Jo's bare feet on that marble hallway floor, and then—*GLOCK!*—that wobbly night table is in the parts it was made with and some of those parts have busted right over Mister Rose's head.

There's a bunch of dents in Mister Rose's Afro now. Usually he tries to part it down the middle. But now there are about *four* parts in that head of his.

Mister Rose hits the alarm pager on his belt and starts walking all wobbly like he just got off one of those upside-down roller coasters and Coly Jo is still trying to make more parts in his Afro with that night table and juvies are mad cheering and whistling through their teeth and then some of those big day guards who stay over by the hash house are busting it up the stairs and popping off on their walkie-talkies. Just like that, they are throwing that armlock on Coly Jo and busting him in the ribs and in the belly and on the back of the head and in other places, too, and Mister Rose is all bugged-out and falling against the wall with that haunted-house look up on his face.

Mister Rose sits in a chair while he watches us bust that A-train. He's still got those funny parts in his Afro, and the way he is slumping in that chair you'd think he had some of Fat Rick's cough syrup.

Every time we pass him at the first floor he counts out our lap and tells us that he will win. He even calls us motherfuckers a few times, and you never hear no one at Hamstock use that word. If you use that word on another juvy you're guaranteed to find yourself in a chuck with the quickness. It's funny how a word can start a chuck like that.

So Mister Rose is sitting all funny in that chair of his and juvies are mad fighting for that Spalding air and busting mouth spit and falling on the stairs.

"I'm gonna win," Mister Rose calls out in that sleepy voice.

After a few hours of the A-train your body just goes to that place that's kind of numb. You start thinking how freaky it is that you can tell the bones in your legs to lift you over the next step. It's kind of funny how the body will move like that even though it feels like it's shutting itself down. You'd be surprised what your body can do on the A-train. You'd be surprised how many times you pass Mister Rose and how the light changes on the window in the stairwell and how freaky the thought of that aurora horn blowing at you in just a few hours is. You'd be surprised at how Boo and Hodge are busting that A-train right along beside you, and how their faces look to you, like they ain't the ones who stuck Demetrius Gord in the side with that pencil. But you know they did it cause you saw them sharpening it together with a grub knife they cribbed from the hash house. You saw them doing it right in their patch when you walked by after slate docket.

But the freakiest part is that you keep busting that A-train cause you feel like if you do it and make it all the way until that aurora horn blows—all the way there—that you'll feel like you've done something *good*, that somehow it's putting you on that *path* that Deacon Bob Fly is always bumping at the gums about.

Coly Jo gets three weeks in the Stink Hole. Slider had to go there twice. They call it the Stink Hole cause all you get is a metal bed and a sink and this nasty-ass toilet full of horseflies. That toilet don't even got no cover, either. According to Slider, they only open your door to give you food and the only face you see is that guard's face who passes you the food.

There ain't no windows and barely any light and you start talking to yourself and pulling your hair out and seeing big spiders on the walls and shit like that.

Slider got sent to the Stink Hole twice while he was at

Hamstock. Once for throwing a rock through a hash house window, and once for putting his hand on this Honey's booty who came to Hamstock to talk to us about safe sex and using those rubber condos. Her name was Miss Blouser and she had one of those booties that's shaped like a Missus Smith apple—at least that's how Slider described it.

Slider only got two days in the Stink Hole for the window and four days for what he did to Miss Blouser. Dean Petty made him write a letter to that woman saying he was sorry, too.

But that's two *days* and four *days*. Most juvies could bust a clip like that. You don't *never* hear of no juvy getting *three weeks* in the Stink Hole, though. Never.

MY NEW PATCH MATE JUST CAME IN. ON my way back from the hash house I saw him getting out of the depot van. He's a white kid with this bugged-out shaved head and he might be the longest juvy you'll ever see at Hamstock, at least six-six. A kid that long with a shaved head makes the head look twice as big. And he walks all hunched over and lazy, too, like one of those old shoeshine guys you see begging for business at the bus station. He's about as bow-legged as it gets, too. He only had to take about ten steps to get from the parking lot to Spalding.

Whenever there's a new opening at Hamstock they fill it up with the quickness. It's like there's always a depot van revving that engine somewhere out past those bean fields, waiting for some kid to get caught at something so they can turn him into a juvy.

They call this kid Long Neck. He might be one of those fire setters or he might be a stick-up kid or he might be a mad tough chucker. You never know about a new juvy.

When I come through the patch hole he stops and looks at me all funny like I got some boogies hanging out of my nose. He's taking my clothes out of the top two drawers. He just stands there with my clothes in his hands and looks at me for a second. Then he starts unpacking his stuff and puts it in the top two drawers. I just play it smooth cause he's new. You got to cut some slack to new juvies.

"I'm Sura," I say. But he just keeps stuffing his shit in my drawers. He ain't even looking at me. He's so long he's even got to bend all low to get to those top two drawers. You've seen grown men who are that long, and sometimes a kid in high school will get long like that, but this kid can't be more than thirteen or they wouldn't stick him on this floor.

"Your real name Long Neck?" I ask, but he just keeps grabbing shit out of his bag and stuffing it in my drawers. I might as well be talking to some bricks.

I stand there for another minute and watch him. Some of my socks have fallen on the floor. He's got about the longest legs you'll ever see on a juvy. And he's got all of these freaky scabs on his lips.

This kid around my way had those scabby lips like that and he used to do this trick where he would ball up his fist and stick the whole thing in his mouth. Those lips got to get mad stretched to do that. I saw him sucking on some butane lighter fluid once, too. And Slider said he saw the same kid mouth-kissing this three-legged German shepherd on his front lawn and the neighbors had to call the fire department.

You got to watch out for kids with those scabby lips like that.

After Long Neck is finished unpacking, he opens up

Coly Jo's bottom drawer and pulls out that unbreakable comb he used to bust those naps with. And then, even though this kid don't got no *hair*, he starts combing his head with it. Only it's more like he's scratching his scalp, and that comb is digging right in, too. You can see the red marks he's making.

Then he puts that comb in his pocket and moves over to the bunk bed and climbs up in *my* bunk and lays up, leaving my clothes all bunched up on top of the dresser.

At first I think he's joking cause he does it so quick. If it was a joke it might be kind of smooth, but the way he is laying up like that, you can tell it ain't no joke at all. He's got that used-up look, like those long limbs are through for the day. He turns his whole body toward the wall.

"That's my bunk, man," I say, but Long Neck just keeps playing like he don't hear me. Then I say it again. I go, "Hey man, you're layin up in my bunk." He still don't flinch so I go, "And those are my clothes. You gonna put em back?" But he just lays up there in my bunk, picking at those scabby lips, so I tell him to have some respect. I go, "Have some respect, man." Then Long Neck turns over and looks at me for a second. On his side, his face looks long, too. That jawbone is like a long letter "L." In fact, every part of his body seems long. Even those eye dots seem long in his long-ass skull. They should call him Long *Body* or Long *Juvy* instead of Long *Neck*.

Then he opens up that scabby mouth and goes, "You wanna fight me for it?" Even his *voice* seems long. Then he kicks his shoes off and rolls back over.

I stand there frozen for a minute and just watch those

long shoes on the floor, at the end of what should be *his* bunk. Then I look over at Coly Jo's desk and see the juvy sheets they issue you when you first get to Hamstock. They got those laundry digits all over them. They probably stick those digits on there like that so they know if a juvy's choking off and getting those sheets stained up.

They try to count everything at Hamstock. Once every few weeks Nurse Rushing asks you how many "bowel movements" you busted that week. They might as well stick some digits on that hash house food so they can count it when it comes out in your shit. You see how they do that kind of stuff in grocery stores. Everything's got a number: canned peas and cereal and fudgsicle pops—all that stuff. Well, everything might as well have a number at Hamstock, too. Even juvy shit.

I walk over and crib those sheets off his desk and make up the bottom bunk. If he's going to lay up in my bed, then I'm going to lay up on his sheets, that's for damn sure.

After blackout I try to tell Long Neck about how Coly Jo and I would bust our blackout shifts, but he just goes, "I don't care what you used to do," and falls asleep.

After it's quiet for a minute I start to think about Coly Jo. You got to wonder how Coly Jo is doing in the Stink Hole. You got to wonder if he's keeping that head together, if he's getting that chocolate milk belly up at all.

Thinking about Coly Jo makes me want to bust a blackout shift with him. I just play like I'm busting my regular blackout shift, and I lay up in my bunk for those fifteen clicks. I even picture Coly Jo in the other bunk, even though it ain't really his no more. Things are going pretty smooth. That faucet down the hall is mad dripping those drips.

For a long time I just concentrate on those drips and clean those thoughts. I even clean those Coly Jo thoughts and just lie still. It gets so smooth that I think I can actually hear the *parts* of the water, and how those water parts break up and make that little splash noise when they hit the bottom of the sink.

But on the sixteenth click my head starts to get mad heavy and my eyes are shutting on their own, and that slow, dreamy lungwind leaking out of Long Neck's mouth ain't helping much. So I roll out of Coly Jo's bunk and sit at my desk and start messing with some math digits.

At first I bust a couple of rows of 3's and I spread them out nice and neat so there's enough room for other digits. When I'm finished busting those rows I stick some titty dots on them. When I got myself a nice batch of bosoms I throw some number 7's in there and get those arms and legs stuck on, and for some reason those number 7's are moving in all of these bugged-out directions so it looks like kicking and punching, like they're kung fu fighting, and before long I got myself a bunch of Honeys who are *chucking*.

They're all up on each other's backs and busting each other in the face and scratching each other in the bosoms, too. I throw some angry "What-did-you-say-to-me!" eye dots on them, too. It gets to be so real that I can even hear some of that kung fu fighting *music* in the background with some flutes and guitars and electric pianos.

Then I start whisper-shouting at the paper. I'm going, "Stop chucking! Stop chucking, goddamnit!"

And after that I start carping them all and sending them to Dean Petty's office to be *paddled*. I use the number 9 to draw Dean Petty and the number 4 to draw that paddle. *Wop . . . wop . . . wop . . .* goes the paddle. Those Honeys are mad clutching their booty-skirts and crying and falling all over his big iron desk.

I got some Honeys busting it at gut drill, too. Those bosoms look good in pushup position. I use an 8 and some 1's to draw Mister Tully. I even draw that raspberry spot on his face with a 0.

I am using so many numbers now that I don't even know what I'm drawing. For a second I just sit there and look at all of that math on the paper. Even some 2's and 6's are mixed up in there and I don't *never* use no 2's or 6's. Man, that shit is mad freaky.

After I look at my digit art for a minute I tear that piece of paper right up and make some paper snow and let that paper snow fall right in the junk can.

When I look up, Long Neck is staring at me from the top bunk. Those long eyes of his are saying, "Shut the fuck up, man!" But mines are saying, "You don't know me from a box of Chiclets, so close those long-ass eyes of yours, Scab Face!"

We look at each other like that for a couple of minutes. I ain't even blinking. I won't look away first. I don't care *how* long he is. He could be longer than that lucky river in Kankakee and I wouldn't care.

You can still hear that faucet dripping those drips.

After some more clicks I take out Hurricane's bust-out map. I look at how he drew the fence and the fields and that wavy line of the road and the trees and those parts beyond the fields that you don't even know about. What's funny is that Hurricane drew it all with some crayons, like when you're about four years old and you're busting a picture of the fire chief for your moms or something.

I used to draw a whole bunch of shit with crayons. Once I drew a picture of this dog playing some checkers and Mazzy sent it off to this magazine and they put it in the magazine. I'm pretty good with the color red.

You can look at a picture sometimes and it'll start to tell a story. Once I looked at this painting of an old lady sitting at a table. She had this crumpled-up paper bag face. There was this rifle set in front of her. The rifle was the only thing on the table. I stared at that painting for a long time and I started seeing that old lady pick that rifle up off the table and walk over to the window all bow-legged and locked up in the joints. Then I saw her making all of these bugged-out faces and mad shouting out, "You stinking hooligan bastards, I'll show you *crazy*! I fought in every war there ever *was*!" And then that old lady started capping off that rifle at a bunch of wild wolfmen guys who were storming her house with some pitchforks and foaming at the mouth and shit. Don't ask me where that came from, but that's what happened when I stared at that painting.

When I look at that stuff on Hurricane's map I start to see myself in a story. I see *myself* climbing that Hamstock fence, and I see myself busting it through the bean fields with those quiet Indian feet, and then I see myself diving into that pond and stopping up my lungwind while some dogs come and try to snuff old Sura out like they do in those fugitive flicks.

Then I see that freight train coming and I blast out of that water and shake the fish out of my pants and I am busting it to those tracks like I am beating another juvy at the rabbit line and those snuff dogs are on my tail with the quickness and those knees are high and those dogs are mad barking and I'm up in the air with some basketball hops and I make that smooth grab for a boxcar—*Go, Sura!*—and then there's nothing but the engine chuffing and darkness and the smell of some coal maybe and then I'm pulling some food I cribbed from the hash house out of my sleeves and grubbing for that vitamin energy and changing trains and hitching some rides on the backs of trucks and walking a lot on dirt roads and shit and then it's like eight or nine days later and I am in a new town where nobody knows me and I get a paper route maybe and live at the YMCA and get back into a school and bust that straight path that Deacon Bob Fly is always bumping at the gums about and there would be this one special Honey with smooth hands who I could tell everything to—the whole nine—and she would be like that Honey in the picture frame on Dean Petty's big iron desk and she would understand and put that smooth hand of hers on old Sura's hair and maybe she would have one of those Mason Pearson brushes that go for about sixty bones at the pharmacy and maybe she would brush through that Sura hair and then maybe she would put that brush down and just use her hand to pet me to sleep . . .

NO ONE CAN BEAT STURM LISTER IN THE crying game. Sturm Lister's got these freaky green eyes and when he cries it looks like they change color, like they go blue or something.

We are in slate docket. Flip Tate and Dorsey Payne are huddled around Sturm's desk. This juvy called Squeaky is going against Sturm. Juvies in slate docket got mad tenths on Sturm. Flip Tate and Dorsey Payne are the only juvies going with Squeaky.

The way the game works is like this: You can't touch your eyes or bite your mouth or nothing like that. You got to keep your hands on your desk and then someone goes *Cry!* The first juvy who cries wins.

Juvies will usually play the crying game when Miss Denton takes her square break after third period. Sometimes you'll see a crying game at the hash house too, but not as often as you'll see one in slate docket.

You only get about three minutes to play. Miss Denton smokes those Merits. Those squares got that nasty label.

I know this kid around my way called Big Walt with this long-ass blond hair who will bust some throw-up if he sees a Merit label. He'll throw up if you say "mustard" and "mayonnaise," too. And he'll throw up if you microwave some baloney and eat it in front of him. Big Walt is funny like that. He says he gets sick from a Merit label cause it looks like a piece of microwaved baloney with mustard on it. Big Walt's cool, though, so you can't do that too much. He's the smartest kid around my way. He can name all of the presidents of the United States and state capitals and shit like that.

So Squeaky and Sturm Lister got their hands on their desks and they're facing each other and Flip Tate and Dorsey Payne are going, "C'mon, Squeaky, just like you did it in the patch. Go, Squeak! Go, boy!"

Squeaky is making all of these bugged-out faces like he is crying, like those faces little kids make when they drop some chocolate cake in a puddle or something, but the funny thing is that there ain't no tears coming out of his eyes. Flip Tate and Dorsey Payne are mad cheering him on, too, like they got a full clip of juvy pounds on the game. But Squeaky just keeps stopping up that lungwind and making those faces.

When you look at Sturm Lister you see those green eyes and that still mouth and it's like he ain't even breathing. It's like he shut himself down and made that heartbeat stop. And you think that there ain't nothing behind those eyes cause his face is so still. But then those eyes get mad glazed with the quickness and that color changes to something like blue and those tears start flowing.

All of the other juvies in slate docket just shake their heads like they knew what was coming all along. Some are even going *Got him another one* and shit like that. It's kind of funny how they say that. It's kind of like how Hodge tells Sham how he got *him* another one when he buffaloes a juvy and starts to put that notch in the tree.

When Miss Denton comes back into slate docket she is rubbing those yellow fingers together. She always comes back into slate docket like that. Those Merits must be mad powerful to make your fingers get to rubbing together like that.

Miss Denton looks over at Sturm Lister and those eyes of hers close up and go mean and she starts going, "What did you do to this boy! What did you *do*!"

When no one says nothing, Miss Denton takes out her notebook and starts carping everyone except Sturm.

You just *know* that Sturm's got that chocolate milk belly up inside. His face is all shiny, and he *looks* sad, but you just *know* that he's thinking about those bones he'll be collecting this Friday and the next Friday and the Friday after that. You just *know* how he's thinking about how thick those juvy pounds will feel in his pocket.

Sometimes Long Neck likes to walk around the patch with a finger gun. And sometimes he'll stand at the window and aim that finger gun and cock his thumb back and close one eye hole like he is capping off at some birds in the sky. When he fires he makes this noise with his scabby lips that sounds like an egg busting on the floor. It's sort of like *"Blop."*

When I walk into the patch he is sitting at my desk.

And he is sporting my black "Dy-no-mite" T-shirt that I sport under my windbreaker when I go roller skating. It's got this mad smooth glitter-gold lettering that catches those Casablanca lights at the rink and gets the Honeys looking.

You got to make sure not to open up your windbreaker too much, though. Otherwise the Honeys will get those flashbulb eyes. You don't want them getting too excited.

Once I opened the front of my windbreaker too much and this Honey with these big horse teeth started chasing me around the rink with her hands outstretched like she wanted to crib those glitter-gold letters right off my shirt. I had to mad hide out in the bathroom and wait for that Honey with the horse teeth to step off.

I saw her at the roller-skating rink a week later and every time I skated by her I had to close up my windbreaker with the quickness. You got to watch out for those Honeys who will chase you like that. Those nonsmooth Honeys with the horse teeth will get those flashbulb eyes and start busting blow-kisses at you and spilling Cokes on themselves and start foaming at the mouth and shit if you ain't careful. They'll wait for you in the parking lot sometimes, too.

So Long Neck is just sitting there at my desk with those scabby lips. Why would he want to wear *my* shirt? I think. It ain't even his size.

"That's my shirt, man," I say. Long Neck just starts stroking those glitter-gold letters with those long, nasty fingers.

"Take it off," I say. But he just keeps stroking those letters. When you look at him from above, that shaved head of his looks all white and veiny, like one of those vulture heads you see in cartoons. He's the kind of kid who would break a camera with the quickness. Even those expensive ones you use on safaris and shit.

"Take it off, man," I say again.

Long Neck throws this ugly-ass smile on his face, and those scabs on his lips get all stretched out like some pus is going to bust out of them. He's mad stretching my shirt out with those with those big bony-ass shoulders of his, too.

Then he stops smiling and says it's *his* shirt and keeps right on stroking those letters. I just stand there for a minute and look at how my shirt looks all small on him. If I stick him in his jaw I bet he'll think twice about cribbing shit out of my drawers.

There's this move Slider showed me where you make a fist and stretch your arm out and lock your elbow so all the bones line up. Then you got yourself a pole. You put your fist right in front of a kid's face and he thinks you're just measuring him off and then you turn that shoulder and—*BLOWWW!*—that kid is hobbling around and reaching for the wall and looking for something soft to fall on. But you got to get those bones mad lined up.

If I line those bones up and stick him while he's sitting down like that, I bet I can get that thumb wrapped around my fist, too, like Slider showed me. You never want to let that thumb pop out when you're throwing a punch. It'll break off with the quickness.

If I hit Long Neck in that soft spot underneath his eye I

bet that that ugly face of his will open up and get bloody, too, like some liquid flowers.

So I lock my elbow and get those bones lined up and then I start to ball up that thumb-wrap and my blood starts cooking and I am looking at those scabs on his lips and I am looking at that sweet spot on his nose and then I close my eyes and see myself busting him with that arm pole cause if you're going to hit a kid you should always see yourself doing it in your mind first.

When I open my eyes, Long Neck is leaning back in his chair and his hand is raised and he starts pointing that finger gun again and cocking that thumb back and jerking that finger gun back like he is shooting at birds again, except he ain't shooting at birds and he ain't shooting at the treehand and he ain't shooting at nothing outside the patch. That finger gun is mad pointed at *me*. *"Blop,"* he says with those scabby lips. *"Blop, blop."*

DEMETRIUS GORD NEVER CAME BACK from the infirmary. That pencil they broke off in his side must have done something mad serious cause he's gone. He didn't even come back to his patch to get his stuff. They just had some guards collect his shit and put it in plastic bags.

You got to wonder what's going to happen to a kid like Demetrius Gord. You got to wonder if he'll always be walking into shower rooms with that sex pole up. You got to wonder if he's always going to be getting stuck with pencils.

A kid like Demetrius Gord should probably sanitize himself alone all the time. He should always bill his shower spot good before he cuts that water on. Either that or he should carry a gun into the shower room.

You can't go through life getting pencils stuck in your side. Your body can only get a hole in it so many times. After a while the blood runs out of that shit that fixes the holes. It gets weak. And when your blood gets weak you wind up a hebofeeliac like Petey Sessoms, and then you spend the rest of your life climbing up in trees.

❧ ❧ ❧

At study box I'm sitting with Long Neck and Flip Tate and this new juvy whose two front teeth are missing. Long Neck keeps picking at those scabby lips and dropping those scab parts on this piece of paper. Then he rolls that paper up like a big straw and holds it above his head and lets those scab parts slide right down the straw and into his mouth hole. After that he takes out Coly Jo's unbreakable comb and starts scratching his scalp with it so you can see those red marks. I just ignore Long Neck and his nasty-ass habits. I just hope he don't get those scab parts all over my Dy-no-mite shirt.

I take out my history book. I got Mazzy's letter stashed in it. I figure you can stash a letter from your moms in your history book and bust a read at study box. You could probably bust two or three reads if Mister Rose is busy grubbing those barbecue potato chips.

Dear Sura,

Today I started fixing up your room. I spent the morning clearing out boxes and washing the floor and putting in a new light fixture. It used to be a storage room and there are some holes in the wall, but we've spackled and cleaned it up. There's a window with this little piece of purple stained glass, and you can see the old train bridge and how the blackbirds nest in it.

Flintlock helped me buy you a new dresser today. It has three drawers. Flintlock said he would help us get you some new clothes, too. By the time you get out you will probably have grown a full size. He said he might even get you your own pair of roller skates. I am planning on wallpapering, too, and putting a rug down.

I am sorry that we can't be together right now, Sura. I miss you very much. I hope that you have been thinking about why you are away. I hope you are sorry for damaging those cars. I hope this is the last time we have to deal with the courts.

I'm sure you are looking forward to going back to regular school. The junior high around here just put in a new cinder track. I know how you've always been a fast runner. The police officer who caught you told me you were one of the fastest kids he's ever had to chase.

Flintlock is looking forward to meeting you. He is a good man who has had a hard life. He fought in the Vietnam War and had some problems for a while, but things have changed for the better. I think you two will get along just fine.

Please try to work with Deacon Bob Fly. He really thinks you have potential. Four months is not a long time. Be good, Sura.

Love,

Mazzy

I picture Mazzy and Flintlock putting up all of that wallpaper in my room and I picture looking at that old train bridge out of that window with the little piece of purple stained glass and how those blackbirds nest in the train bridge and I picture Flintlock and Mazzy maybe buying me some roller skates and I think how I would like those Bally speed skates with the neon wheels and how the ball bearings in those wheels make that smooth spinning sound and I think about how four months ain't so long and how the snow will be on the ground and how the trees will be all white like they got that cake mix on their branches and I think about how living in a house might be pretty smooth for once and how those YMCA rooms make you feel all funny like your life is in too many parts like it's a TV that gets fixed but never seems to work right again and I think how maybe busting out ain't such a good idea . . .

When I look up, Long Neck is wiping his fingers all over my Dy-no-mite shirt again. Then he looks at me with that long face and that shaved head and smiles and points at Mazzy's letter with Coly Jo's unbreakable comb, like he was reading it right along with me.

The problem with those long juvies is that they can stretch their damn necks all over the place.

When a juvy cribs a grub knife from the hash house you know he's got something heavy on his head. You see it every once in a while, how he'll get that haunted-house look up on his face like some boogymonsters are creeping up behind him, and how he'll put those Indian feet on so it looks like he's got those night creeping thoughts.

If you get caught cribbing *anything* from the hash house those day guards will have you walking so many carp circles it'll feel like you got a bunch of pennies in the floors of your shoes.

The most non-smooth part about cribbing a grub knife is sticking it down your drawers so it stays all tucked in right. A grub knife moving around in some drawers can get to be mad dangerous. A quick bow in the side or some sweat can set that grub knife loose and get your lungwind up with the quickness.

If you were to use math to describe what might happen, you'd have to picture the number 1. But that number 1 might be bent funny and it might have a little piece of the middle missing. Picture that. Damn, that's some freaky shit.

Tonight at the hash house I heard something mad strange. Dorsey Payne and this new juvy they call Shanky were sitting at a table next to mines. Shanky was bumping at the gums about this kid from around his way who knows Boo Boxfoot.

This kid who knows Boo told Shanky that Boo could have gotten out of Hamstock four months ago. He said that his charge was reversed, that the courts found out that it was actually one of his *boys* who blinded that old lady with that crowbar.

So Shanky was telling Dorsey Payne about how Boo had

to go to Dean Petty's office to get those release forms but that he wouldn't do it; that Mister Rose and two day guards had to throw that armlock on him and *drag* him there.

And when he got there Boo asked Dean Petty to let him *stay*. In front of his moms and everything. According to Shanky, Boo's moms was pulling on his arm and begging him to come home, but Boo just begged back to Dean Petty that he wanted to stay. In fact, Boo smashed up some shit in Dean Petty's office too, so he would get *carped*.

Dorsey Payne just kept going, "Stop lyin, Shanky. Stop lyin."

You could just see Boo doing that, too. Everything gets all reversed with a juvy like Boo.

And you just *know* when the time comes again for Boo to go to Dean Petty's office for those release papers that he's just going to bust up some more shit. Maybe that's why that buffaloing is always so heavy on his head—so he can get that ass carped some more. Maybe that's why he slung that bucket of shitblobs all over Coly Jo.

You would figure that a kid like Boo Boxfoot ain't afraid of nothing; that those chucking skills and that man-strength would make things mad easy for him no matter where he was at.

You would figure that Boo Boxfoot ain't afraid to go back to his own *home* with his own *moms*. And his moms must be mad blabbermouthing that shit all around her way, too. How else would Shanky know?

Man, that's bugged-out.

Juvies are mad busting it back to Spalding to get those three clicks' worth of floor hockey. I'm so tired I just want to go back to my patch and lay up in Coly Jo's bunk for those three clicks.

But when I get to Spalding juvies ain't going inside to play floor hockey at all. They are all cheering in front of the dead tree, and by the way those cheers sound you just know that there's some chucking going on.

Hodge's shirt is off and he's got my new patch mate all headlocked and those big arms of his are balled up like some giant marbles. His skin is all shiny, too, like that blood's been cooked for chucking.

Long Neck's face is mad purple and those scabby lips look like they are going to bust some pus.

Part of old Sura thinks this is pretty smooth, that Long Neck's finally got what's coming to him. He ain't looking so *long* now with his face all purple and Hodge talking to Sham while he's beating him, like Sham is right there leaning up against the tree.

Long Neck ain't looking so *long* now with that hand of his hitting the ground like that, like he thinks that tree dirt is going to help him somehow. He might think twice about cribbing shit out of juvies' drawers and wearing it around Hamstock. He might think twice about laying up in other juvies' bunks, too. Maybe he'll start having some respect for his patch mate.

Hodge finally lets him go and Long Neck rolls on his back and grabs at his neck and tries to catch his lungwind and those long legs are mad kicking out. It's funny how his face is all purple but his head is still white like a buzzard.

Hodge puts his shirt back on and pulls his hash spoon out of a pocket and starts to carve that new buffalo notch next to his initials. It's kind of funny how Hodge can just pull out that hash spoon, like every time he does it those day guards are working on crossword puzzles or something. It ain't like he tries to keep it tucked in his shorts all secret-like, the way I've been keeping my grub knife. He just pulls it out of his pocket.

Hodge wipes some of that sweat off his face and kind of smiles and starts telling Sham how he got him another one.

I AM LAYING UP IN COLY JO'S BUNK WHEN Long Neck comes hobbling in. He stands in the center of the patch for a minute. He's got that haunted-house look up on his face and those long fingers are rubbing at that neck.

He sits down at his desk and keeps right on rubbing his neck, like he can't get Hodge's choke-hold rubbed out of it. You can hear that lungwind mad stopping up and leaking out. He opens Coly Jo's desk drawer a few times and then closes it like he don't know what to do.

I think he might be crying cause that lungwind is seized up now and that patch air is cutting in and out of his nose like there's a boogydance on his face. Those big bony shoulders of his are mad bobbing up and down, too.

I can't stand seeing such a long kid busting a cry like that. It's like when you see a little kid fall down in a mud puddle and he's maybe got a kite in his hand and that kite breaks and he starts crying or shits his drawers or something. I can't stand that stuff.

"At least you didn't climb up in the tree," I say. I don't

know why I say that, especially after he cribbed my Dy-no-mite shirt and laid up in my bunk and pointed that finger gun at me—especially after all that.

My Dy-no-mite shirt is all torn up in the back. Some of those glitter-gold letters are missing, too.

"Most juvies don't even want to fight him," I say. He is still rubbing his neck and smoothing out his lungwind. Damn, that's one of the reddest necks you'll ever see.

"Most juvies just reach for that lowest branch and start climbin," I say.

Long Neck opens and closes that drawer a few more times. The funny thing is that he ain't even *looking* in it. It's more like he's *testing* it or something.

Then he stops and opens that desk drawer wide and lays that long hand over the edge and—*BLAM*—closes the drawer on his hand.

The night guard left today. His replacement is this old guy with these thick pop-bottle glasses. From your patch window you can't even see nothing behind them. He walks around Hamstock all soft and careful like he's got that hiplock, and he don't even bust those clicks on the hitch-post when he makes his rounds. Tonight Mister Rose had to use a stopwatch to bill out those three clicks' worth of free time.

In fact, this new guy don't even use a ribstick. Instead of a ribstick he carries this leather rope. And from your patch window he looks like a *Honey* swinging a *purse* or something, like he's singing some of those old dog booty Lawrence Welk songs you hear when you're hanging with some senior citizens.

You can just see an old guy doing that, too. You can just see him whistling some of those songs and getting all light in the pants. Those are the kind of guys who walk around and whistle those old movie songs and dance with brooms and shit. Those are the kind of guys who soak in the bubble bath a little too long.

So I'm watching the new night guard out of the patch window and Long Neck is laying up in my bunk. Those big feet of his are mad hanging off the end, too.

After the new night guard steps off around the infirmary I sit down and take out my history book and study Hurricane's bust-out map. I got that grub knife right up against my leg, too, just in case. A juvy like Long Neck will get beat by Hodge and get that lungwind all stopped up and then out of nowhere he'll pounce on you and start a chuck just cause he got beat. When you lose some gum the first thing you want to do is go crib some more from the pharmacy on Choate Street and get that flavor back up in your mouth.

So I am looking at that tractor shed and that pond and I am using some math to bill the distance from the pond to the train tracks, and I am trying to figure out how long it will take me to get from the shed to the tracks. Hurricane wrote down that it's about three lengths of the parking lot, which means I could probably bust that distance in under forty seconds. Suddenly Long Neck rolls over in my bunk. I pull that grub knife into my leg with the quickness.

"Can I go with you?" he says.

"Huh?"

"When you break out . . ." Long Neck says. "Can I go too?"

I don't say nothing. I just stare at that vulture head of his.

"I saw the map," Long Neck says. When Long Neck talks, his mouth moves all fast, like the thoughts in his head are all stopped up. Those scabs on his lips get all stuck together, too.

"Man, you got some nerve," I say.

"I know how to make booby traps," he says.

"You got no respect," I say.

"I can hot-wire a car, too," Long Neck says.

"So," I say.

"I blew up a mailbox," he says, mad picking at his fingers. That's about the dumbest thing you'll ever hear a juvy do. I thought Dorsey Payne cribbing that Thanksgiving turkey out of that cop car was stupid. But this mailbox story wins the Dog Booty Trophy.

Slider and I only gave out the Dog Booty Trophy two times. Once this kid named Jeebo ate a whole box of pencils cause we told him it would make his sex pole bigger. He wound up throwing up all over this Honey after he got in her drawers and he had to lay up in bed for two days and piss in a cup and drink cod liver oil.

The other time we gave out the Dog Booty Trophy was after Bunky tried to set his fart on fire with a lighter. He had the flame dial on too high and set his pants on fire and he had to jump into the junkpond over on Fourth Street.

So you get the Dog Booty Trophy if you do shit like

that. You can make a Dog Booty Trophy out of a canned ham and some popsicle sticks.

We are quiet for a minute. Long Neck takes Coly Jo's unbreakable comb out and starts scratching his head again.

I picture Long Neck holding his Dog Booty Trophy. The problem with that, though, is he'd probably eat the piece of ham that's supposed to be the dog booty.

"It's a federal offense, you know," he says, still scratching his head.

"What is?" I ask.

"Blowing up a mailbox."

"Sounds pretty stupid," I say.

"It's government property."

I've let up some on that grub knife. I've let it drop on the chair.

"They had to surround me," Long Neck says. "You ever been surrounded before?"

"Big deal," I say.

"They put a three-point stance on you and everything. Ever see that?" he asks, like that really means something.

"Why would you wanna blow up a mailbox?" I say.

"It was either that or the bowling alley," he says.

I don't say nothing else. For some reason I picture us busting it from that tractor shed to the train tracks. I'm way out in front of him and those snuff dogs are mad on our tails. Then I'm at the gravel where they lay the tracks and I make that jump onto a boxcar and I pull myself in through the sliding door and it's dark and there's the smell of coal and that coal dust is all in my face and hair and I wipe it off and look back and Long Neck is on his knees in some weeds and those snuff dogs are all over him.

"I want my shirt back," I tell him. "I want it back now."

"Yeah. Yeah, sure," he says.

Long Neck slips out of his bunk and pulls my shirt out of his laundry bag and hands it to me.

"Some letters got ripped off," he says.

When he stands in front of me you can see that he's got one of those caved-in chests. He's probably one of those kids in gym class who always gets blasted in dodgeball. You can just see those balls coming at him and his bony-ass back all pressed up against the bleachers and his hands out in front of his face.

I take my shirt. There's some of that scabby shit on it. He probably wiped his boogies all over it, too. And now he wants to bust out of here with me.

Damn, that's messed up.

"And I want my bunk back, too," I say.

Long Neck turns around and tilts that vulture head of his a little and slips into Coly Jo's bunk. Just before he lays up for good he picks at his face some and then he blows this mad underwater-sounding fart that smells like one of those liverwurst sandwiches that's been in the sun too long. I can't imagine how many of those he's busted in my bunk. He's been laying up in it for almost two weeks now.

"If you were smart you would start busting some blackout shifts with me," I tell him.

Long Neck says okay.

I slip that grub knife down my leg and into my sock and

climb back up into my bunk. It's smooth how you can feel the way your bunk fits to your body. A body can lay up on a bunk like that and that bunk will form to it. Shoes will do that, too. "It's good to be back," I say to my bunk with my mind. I just hope there ain't none of that scabby shit all stashed in my pillow.

I explain the blackout shifts and he keeps going "Okay" like everything's smooth, and then we are quiet for a while. Maybe this juvy ain't so bad after all, I think.

That patch hole light is electric now. You can hear Mister Rose busting his blackout sweep.

After it's quiet for a minute I start to think about Coly Jo again. You got to wonder if that guard who slides him his food is maybe talking to him and saying hello and shit. You got to wonder if he maybe gets a towel or something to throw over the parts in his metal bed so it don't cut into his back. You got to wonder if he's still dropping that hand of his over his belly. You got to wonder if he's crying into the back of his elbow like he used to do in the patch.

After Mister Rose makes his blackout sweep and those Dr. J's squeak on down the stairs, Long Neck turns in his bunk and whispers at me.

He goes, "Hey, Sura."

"What?" I whisper back.

Then Long Neck laughs a little and I go "What?" again and then he stops laughing and tells me how he could show me twelve different ways to kill someone with that grub knife I'm keeping in my sock.

WHEN YOU SHADOW SOMEONE AT NIGHT it's different from shadowing him during the day. During the day you can shadow him and walk like you're walking to a store or around the block or behind the bowling alley or something. But at night when you shadow him, you walk with your shoulders all hunched up and you start tiptoeing like some of that smooth *Pink Panther* music is playing. It's like the night's got some spies hanging out in the trees or something.

It's after blackout. Fat Rick was sleeping at his desk again. When I passed him you could smell that cough syrup thick in the stairwell.

I am shadowing the new night guard and he is swinging his leather rope and whistling some of those bubble bath songs. It's getting cold out and my breath is mad smoking up and you can feel how the ground is making itself hard for winter.

I used to shadow this old man who drove a Benzo. I had to sneak into this rich neighborhood called Good Oaks. Good Oaks is full of rich people and most of them got those fancy foreign rides. This old guy had a '75

Benzo 280 and that hoody was about the smoothest hoody you'll ever see.

I had been billing that spot for a couple of weeks and I knew all about that old guy. I knew how he went golfing on Saturdays and took the top down on Sundays if it was nice and how he'd sport this fancy sweatsuit and walk around the neighborhood and check his watch and bill that heartbeat on his wrist. Some nights he'd stick his Benzo in the garage and some nights he wouldn't.

So I shadowed that guy for a couple of weeks and one time he went on one of his heartbeat walks and I busted it toward his driveway and clipped his hoody. It's the only hoody I ain't sold yet. This kid offered me seventy bones for it but I told him to step off.

I ain't never selling that hoody. Sometimes I just take it out of my hoody bag and watch how the light sparkles off it.

But most of that shadowing happened during the day. Those night spies ain't in the trees during the day.

The night guard disappears behind the gymnasium. I put on those extra-strength Indian feet and shadow him. If you're going to bust out of Hamstock you got to make a break for that fence. And if you're going to make a break for that fence you better know what kind of moves that night guard is going to make.

You got to watch how close he gets to the fence. And you got to know how he will move if he hears a noise. Does he move toward the noise or away from the noise? How fast is he? Does he call for help on his radio right away or does he wait? Shit like that is important.

I pick up a rock. When I get that night guard in my sights

again I throw that rock and it hits the side of the gymnasium. The night guard turns around and I duck behind some bushes. I'm careful so they don't shake. I'm pretty smooth at that kind of shit. I'm good at carnival games, too.

As soon as he hears that rock the night guard makes a fist and starts wrapping that leather rope all around it. He starts to walk toward me. He is about forty feet away now. I am frozen. It's like someone's covered me with that kung fu housecoat with the powers.

If he catches me I'll get the Stink Hole for sure. And I'll probably get another month added to my clip.

He's twenty feet away now. What's freaky is you still can't see his eyes behind those thick glasses. But the way he's walking it's like he *knows* that I'm hiding in the bushes. Like he can smell me or something. Like he's got an Indian *nose* or something. You hear about that sometimes, about how someone can breathe with their eyes or smell stuff with their hands and shit like that. You got to watch out for that. Those are the types of people who will take advantage of you, just cause they got those extra parts in their brains.

I close my eyes tight and pray that he will stop walking.

Then there is the sound of another rock hitting the wall of the gymnasium and the night guard spins around and is mad busting it toward that sound. He disappears around the other side of the gymnasium. I shake off that kung fu housecoat and unfreeze myself and put those extra-strength Indian feet back on and bust it back to Spalding.

When I get back into my patch Long Neck is in Coly Jo's bunk breathing those deep breaths. I climb up in my bunk and lay up and try to smooth out my lungwind.

There ain't no way I'm going to be able to sleep tonight. All of that freezing and unfreezing and shit makes you start to think too fast and get those fire-hands.

I can't figure out where that other rock came from. Maybe it was an old piece of the gymnasium that fell off and hit the side. Or it could have been some hot water pipes busting or something. Pipes will do that when it starts to get cold out. They got to stretch themselves out for those bigger hot water parts. Hot water parts are bigger than cold water parts cause of the boiling.

Just when I am about to close my eyes, Long Neck turns in Coly Jo's bunk and whispers something. It sounds like he is talking in his sleep.

"Huh?" I say. But when he says it again I know he ain't talking in his sleep.

He goes, "Pretty good throw, huh?"

IT SEEMS LIKE EVERY TIME YOU TURN around it's the night again. That's what happens when those trees lose their leaves and the sun gets weak. That's what happens when that air turns cold on you, like it gets stored in a big basement for half the year and then some janitor with a dice habit gets paid off to open that door. That air sneaks up on you with the quickness and gets into those bones and the sun is too weak to cook those bones back up.

It's after blackout and I'm watching the treehand out the window. The wind is tugging on it pretty strong tonight. Mister Rose ain't made his final sweep yet.

Long Neck tells me about his fake eye, how you can tell it's fake by looking at it in the light cause one eye dot gets smaller and the other one stays the same. He shows me in front of his desk lamp and when I come up close those scabby lips look about as nasty as it gets. I should probably tell him about that kid who sucks on lighter fluid and sticks his fist in his mouth and kisses German shepherds and shit. I should probably tell him how the fire department came and took him away.

When Long Neck tilts his head back to show me his eyes, those boogies are mad clogging up his nostrils. That breath of his don't smell too smooth, either, like he grubbed on some athlete's foot or something. That rotten breath of his will make your eyes water with the quickness.

After he shows me his eyes, we climb back into our bunks.

"How'd it happen?" I ask.

"One part of the eye got torn away from another part," he says.

"You got poked?" I ask.

"No."

"Punched?"

"No."

"Rubber band?" I ask. You always hear about how a kid gets busted in the eye with a rubber band. That happens all the time. In slate docket Miss Denton is always telling you not to mess with rubber bands.

"I didn't get the TV fixed," Long Neck says.

"*Oh,*" I say, although I ain't hip to what he's talking about.

"I can fix anything. Toasters. Fans. Radios are easy. But I couldn't fix the TV because it needed a new circuit board and the parts store was closed."

"Damn," I say.

"Yeah. So he comes home and kicks me in the head."

"Who?" I ask.

"My dad," he says.

"He *kicked* you?" I say.

"Yep."

"In the *head*?"

"Right in the eye," he says.

"Your *pops*?"

"He was pretty tanked."

"Damn," I say again.

You hear a lot of stories about a kid getting thrown around by his pops. Sometimes you hear about a belt or a stick. Once I heard about this kid around my way whose pops beat him with a *radio alarm clock*. He kept busting him in the ass with it and the snooze bar kept going off. That kid won't even listen to the *radio* no more. And if we're just slinging some craps or hanging out around my way and someone walks up with a radio, he'll mad bust it back to his house like he's getting chased by a tornado. That's about as messed up as it gets. But you never hear about no kid getting *kicked in the eye* by his own *pops*. You *never* hear about that.

"I'm gonna shoot him," Long Neck says, and he says it all simple, too. He could have said "I'm gonna shoot *dice*" or "I'm gonna shoot some *hoops*" just the same. That's probably why he's always walking around the patch with that finger gun cocked and ready. He's just practicing for his pops.

"I'm gonna shoot him in the eye," he adds.

"Damn," I say again. I say *Damn* a lot. At least it ain't one of those non-words like Ock. At least they say *Damn* in movies and shit.

"Yeah," Long Neck says. "Fucking mailman." Damn, that's a freaky thing to say.

Long Neck is biting his nails now. You can hear those

big teeth of his clopping together like some horse feet.

"You got a gun?" I ask.

"I made one," he says.

"You *made* one?"

"Yeah, I made it. I read a book. It fires twenty-twos," he says. "I read a book," he says again.

You can hear Mister Rose down by the end of the hall. He's got some juvy busting pushups. That juvy counts out his twenty and Mister Rose tells him to get back into his bunk and that if he hears him talking after blackout again he's gonna have his ass busting stair laps. Then that juvy says *Yes sir, Mister Rose* and you can hear that juvy's feet mad shuffling back through his patch hole.

"Hey, Long Neck," I whisper. He don't say nothing back. He just turns in his bunk a little. The thing about sleeping in the top bunk is that you always get stuck looking at the ceiling. And you get to reading the cracks and the paint bubbles and stuff like that, and a crack or a paint bubble can get to looking mad depressing. If you catch yourself looking too long you got to shift those thoughts to something else.

"Hey, man," I whisper again, but he's out. Those long kids can fall asleep like that with the quickness. Once those sleeping parts of the blood smooth out and float to the many parts of the body, your head will go all heavy and warm. I guess with those long kids your head goes twice as heavy and twice as warm.

That lungwind of his is already smoothed out. That lungwind of his is mad long, too. I decide to say it anyway, though.

"Thanks for throwing that rock," I say.

You can hear Mister Rose coming closer with those squeaky-ass Dr. J's. For some reason when you hear those squeaks it's like the hallway starts to disappear and you got to close your eyes. I don't know why you do that. Somehow closing your eyes makes you quieter. Somehow it makes your patch stop breathing.

ON MY WAY TO SLATE DOCKET BOO COMES up to me and pokes me in the chest and tells me that I still got to give him half my juvy pound on Friday. He says he can forget about the *silly mistake* by the fire doors, that he allows a *silly mistake* here and there. He also says that the silly mistake at the fire doors took care of "here" and "there."

He's sporting Coly Jo's squirrel-skin cap again. I swear, if a kid had some wristbands on and he was dead in a body-box, Boo would probably walk right up to that body-box and crib those wristbands.

He tells me I can either pay him that six tenths or get a toe broken. He tells me how he'll break it with some pliers that the Mop Man gave him today; how he won't even bend my toe; how he'll just squeeze it with those pliers until the bone pops. He tells me I won't run so fast with a broken toe.

Deacon Bob Fly is flashing splot cards in front of me. After he flashes the splot card I got to attach a name to each card. The rule about splot cards is that you got to say the first thing that comes into your head. The funny thing is that the pictures on the splot cards ain't really pictures of *nothing*; they're just a bunch of *splots*. They're just a bunch of non-pictures.

Deacon Bob Fly drums those fingers on his desk for a minute and flips a splot card.

". . . Chocolate on the floor," I say.

He looks up and flips another one.

"Motor oil," I say.

He flips again.

"Magic marker on some bread."

He writes something and flips.

". . . Smashed cake . . ."

He looks again and flips.

"Dogshit."

He looks at the card and then up again and then back at the card and flips.

"Cupcake on a window."

He makes a face like something is in his eye and flips.

"Bigfoot on a bike," I say.

He writes something down in his notebook. He flips.

". . . Smaller dogshit . . ."

He stops and looks at me for a minute.

"Sura, let's try and get away from the slop for a minute."

"But that's what I see, man," I say.

"No more slop," he says.

Deacon Bob's got a lot of nerve talking to *me* about *slop*. He's the one who's always getting mad descriptive about that goonfish in that story he's always bumping at the gums about—about how it's got all of these horse teeth and how those horse teeth got mad lake boogies and fisherman guts and athlete's foot and shit all over them.

"Let's try some more," he says.

He flips another card and it looks like a turkey that got smashed by an ice cream truck, but I don't say that. Instead, I go, "Dark cloud," and Deacon Bob goes, "That's better."

He flips another one. It looks like somebody's underarm with a bunch of horseflies on it, but I don't say that either. Instead, I go, "Mess of pain," and Deacon Bob goes, "Now we're talkin," and is mad writing stuff down.

But the next one he flips makes my head feel all heavy. That splot card is like a *body*. And that body is all twisted up and afraid-looking, like someone is beating that body with a whipping stick. And when you look at it real close and think about it for a second, you realize that it looks like *Coly Jo's* body, how his body might look if he was in the Stink Hole and one of those guards was standing over him with a whipping stick or a blackjack or a broom handle or something. That kind of thing will make your head go heavy with the quickness.

"What is it, Sura?" Deacon Bob asks. I don't know what to say. It's like someone has sprayed my mind with a bunch of paint. Every time a word tries to creep into my head it gets cleaned with the quickness.

Then Deacon Bob pushes his big yellow head forward and that pen in his hand jerks up like his hand is ready to write stuff. I hate how he does that. I hate how that notebook's got all of that shit in it about me. I hate how he just opens it up and reads some words and plays like he *knows* me. That notebook might as well have a *picture* of me on the front of it.

You can't just bill someone like that. You can't just open up a notebook and read some chicken scratch and play like you *know* that person. He don't know me from a box of tube socks.

Deacon Bob Fly pushes that splot card right in front of my nose. You can almost see Coly Jo's *face* in it, I swear.

And then it comes to me. That white paint in my head's got a word on it now. I should have thought of it right off.

"What do you see, Sura?" Deacon Bob asks.

It's funny how a splot card can lock your head up like that. It ain't nothing special. It's just a card with a splot on it.

"Sura . . . ?" he says again.

Then I say it. I go, "Kung fu dog."

Deacon Bob Fly just looks at me. That pen in his hand ain't moving at all. It's like he's frozen by that kung fu housecoat with the powers; like someone threw it over that butterfly collar and locked him up.

He don't even know how to write what I've said.

Dear Mazzy,

I read your letter. I put it in my history book. I keep it in there cause juvies don't crib nothing from books cause they don't like books. If I had a hundred bones I could put it in my history book and it would be safe, I swear.

The other day I beat this kid called Chuckie Steptoe in a race. He thought he was slick with his froglegs and his shag-carpeted glasses, but I dusted him good. I'm still undefeated.

My patch mate got sent down to the Stink Hole for trying to bust some furniture over Mister Rose's head. He's been gone for a couple of weeks. He was my best friend. He cried sometimes but he was cool. The Stink Hole is the worst place you can go.

My new patch mate is bugged-out. He's taller than everyone. He's like six-six and he's got lip problems. He exploded a mailbox and got surrounded by some cops. He said they put a three-point stance on him and everything. He says he wants to shoot his pops in the eye.

When I get out, if I live with you and Flintlock, are we going to leave again after a while? Does he keep blow-pops in the freezer? Can he fight? Does he want to marry you?

I ain't too crazy about going back to the YMCA. There are too many old guys with hairy shoulders there.

Does Flintlock know about speed skates? Bally makes the best speed skates. The ones with the neon wheels are the smoothest ones. If he was in a war, how old is he? Is he seventy? Does he got scars on his face? Does he carry a gun? Does he carry two guns? Does he snap out and yell *Fire in the hole* and junk like that? Does he got a fake leg?

I busted some splot cards with Deacon Bob today. One looked like some smashed cake.

I got a thought about what you said in your letter. I ain't going to mess with no more cars, I promise. But don't worry about me. I ain't scared and I don't cry or nothing. I just want to come home.

Love,

Sura

AT JUVY POUND LINE BOO AND HODGE are standing in front and in back of me. Hodge is in front of me. Boo is in back. They made Chuckie Steptoe and that new juvy with no front teeth move to the end of the line.

I think about getting my toe broken with those pliers Boo was talking about. I wonder how much it hurts to get your toebone popped like that. I saw this old man with a broken toe once. He was wearing some sandals and that toe was all crooked and separated from the joint. He walked like he had some mashed potatoes in his drawers, too.

The line starts moving and juvies are getting their tenths and full pounds and stepping off toward the fire doors. Hodge steps up to the window and collects his juvy pound. Now it's my turn.

The Honey at the window flips through her carp book and checks those digits and then pushes my full bone-and-twenty at me and I make a fist over it and step off to the fire doors.

Hodge is standing in front of the fire doors with those

big shoulders of his. When I turn around, Boo is already there, right behind me, like a boogymonster who can walk through a wall.

"Give it up, Sura," he says. I just look at him for a second. I look at his face and I look at the part where his Afro might start if he had an Afro and I look at that little scar on his lip where his mouth sticks. I can't imagine Boo Boxfoot ever being a little kid. In fact, Boo Boxfoot was probably never even born. He probably came from something else, like the trunk of a ride or a junkyard or a cesspool or something. Whatever it was, he came walking out of it with that man-strength and those big hands and that harelip all stuck up on his face; just like he is now, I'd bet you.

"What am I payin for?" I ask. Boo and Hodge look at each other and laugh. "That night table is busted," I say.

"What's he payin for, Ock?" Boo asks Hodge.

"I ain't hip, Ock," Hodge says back to Boo.

Then Boo looks at me with a big, stupid smile on his face and goes, "You're payin for your toe, Sura." Then he laughs again. Hodge laughs, too. Then Boo points to my fist like he knew it was there all along. I lift my fist up in front of Boo, and Hodge undoes my fingers, and I drop my bone-and-twenty into Boo's big, flat-ass palm. Then Boo reaches into his back pocket and gives me six tenths back and a piece of paper all folded up small and says, "That's what you're payin for." Then he goes, "Let's go, Ock," and Boo and Hodge step off back to Spalding.

It's funny how a juvy will crib your juvy pound from you and then give you some tenths back—like handing you some change makes the cribbing part all right.

When I can see that they've stepped off I unfold that piece of paper. You'd think there'd be some kind of new rule on that paper, something about your juvy pound or the dead tree or the hash house line or something, but it ain't nothing like that.

It's a drawing of that night table with *Six tenths* written on the top of it.

Everyone is walking back to Spalding after third hash when two day guards walk by us toting a juvy. When they get close enough you can see that juvy they're toting is Coly Jo. They got his arm all twisted up behind his back and are telling us to move along.

The non-look on Coly Jo's face is the most non-looking non-look you'll ever see. You can see how his baldy ain't no baldy no more, how some of that Afro hair is starting to grow back in. It's more like a *half*-baldy.

A bunch of juvies are saying his name under their breath. They're going *Coly Jo, Coly Jo.* And the way they are saying it makes it sound like they *forgot* about him or something.

It's like when a kid around your way moves to another town and you forget about him and then he moves back around your way cause the other town shut down or something. A town will shut down like that sometimes. It'll get blasted with a tornado and the parts of the town that make it a place to live fly off into the sky and then it becomes a non-town. That's what it's like when you see Coly Jo.

I try saying *Hey, man* to him with my eyes, but he can't

see me cause they got his arm twisted up behind his back and he's too busy looking down.

They stick Coly Jo in an isolation room on the second floor of Spalding. They say that that juvy ghost lives down on the second floor. They say you can hear him slobbering and stuff if you stay up late and it's quiet. They say he'll just show up in your room and look with that paint coming out of his mouth and those spacy eyes and then disappear through a door like some steam. Sometimes they'll stick a juvy in an isolation room if he gets some chicken pops or something and they don't want it spreading. And sometimes they'll stick a juvy in an isolation room if he has a chuck with his patch mate.

After blackout I watch out of the window and see that night guard pass a few times and I put on my Indian feet and grab my windbreaker and walk down to Coly Jo's isolation room.

That hallway on the second floor is mad breathing. His room is all the way at the end, too, and I am walking through all of that hall breath.

The isolation rooms don't got no patch holes. They just got door spaces with curtains.

Fat Rick is supposed to be watching the second floor on a TV that's on his desk. But you just *know* that he's had about four gallons of that cough syrup.

I push the curtain aside and step in. There is only one bed. It looks like a hospital room. Coly Jo is sleeping with his knees tucked into his chest. When he breathes he breathes through his nose holes, but you can't hear his lungwind. It's the most silent breathing you've ever heard. I ain't never watched him sleep before. I've *heard* him breathing that cave breath he would get sometimes, but I ain't never *watched* him.

There's a place where you go behind your eyes sometimes. It ain't like dreaming and it ain't like thinking and it ain't where you go when you're listening to some music. It's a place you go to wait for that boat that picks you up and takes you through your bloodstream to the parts of the mind that make you dream. It happens before you dream but after you fall asleep.

Being in that boat is the safest place you can be, I swear, cause even though you can have a smooth dream about a Honey and wake up with that smile on your face, sometimes you can have a non-smooth dream about a cop or falling out of a building or running in some quicksand and shit like that. So that bloodstream boat is even safer than a dream.

You can bet that that's where Coly Jo is right now. You can just tell by looking at his face. It's kind of like he's got that chocolate milk belly up. That little bloodstream boat is mad floating and about to drop him off in a dream.

I crouch low by the side of his bed. That half-baldy's got a new Afro growing on it. The moonlight from the window passes over his face and makes him look old.

I shake Coly Jo's shoulder a few times and he opens his eyes. Then he closes them and I shake his shoulder again and he opens them wider.

"Hey, man," I whisper.

"Sura?"

"Hey, man," I say again. I am smiling like a little kid. I know that ain't too smooth but I don't care. I put my hand right up on his scratchy half-baldy. "I brought you this," I tell him. Then I fold my windbreaker and put it up on his stomach. Coly Jo puts his hand on it. It's the same hand he used to always hang over that belly of his.

"Ain't seen you in the longest, Sura," he says. His voice sounds all sleepy.

"I know, man," I say. Then Coly Jo closes his eyes for a minute and opens them.

"I'm goin away, Sura," Coly Jo whispers.

"Where?" I say.

"I gotta go away," he says again. Then Coly Jo closes his eyes for a minute but I shake his shoulder.

"Coly Jo," I whisper. "Coly Jo!" He opens his eyes again.

"Where you goin?" I ask.

"They's transferring me," he says.

"Why?" I say.

"They's sending me down."

"Kankakee?" I say.

Coly Jo shakes his head a few times and makes his eyes all big.

"Where they sending you?" I say.

Then Coly Jo swallows something in his throat and goes, "St. Chuck's."

"Damn, man," I say. The white parts in Coly Jo's eyes look like they got bigger, like there wasn't no light in the Stink Hole.

"I'm leaving tomorrow," Coly Jo whispers.

"Damn," I say again. Now I am petting his half-baldy.

"I don't wanna go, Sura," Coly Jo says. "They got that electricity fence down there."

"Don't worry about that, Coly Jo," I say. "Just keep your head."

"I'm skeered, Sura."

"Keep your head, man," I say. I am pulling on his arm, too.

Coly Jo closes his eyes again. I shake his shoulder again and he opens them back up.

"Coly Jo, listen to me," I say. I shake his shoulder a little when I talk cause I don't want him to slip off onto that bloodstream boat again. "I'm bustin out of here, Coly Jo," I say. "You can go with me just like we planned."

"You can't climb no electricity fence, Sura," he says. His voice is mad sleepy. It don't even sound like his voice. It sounds like someone else's voice. Like those day guards at the Stink Hole did something to him. Like they put some drugs in his food or something.

"Come on, man," I say. I am really shaking his shoulder now but it feels all heavy and rubbery. "We can go tonight," I say. Coly Jo closes his eyes again.

"Coly Jo!" I whisper. Those eyes open up about halfway. "I've been watching the new night guard and everything," I tell him. "I shadowed him."

But then Coly Jo's eyes close again and he's on that boat. His lungwind is mad smooth now, too. You can't wake a kid up when he gets like that. You just can't.

I watch him sleep for three or four clicks. You got to

count the clicks in your head. You got to count them in your head when there ain't no ribstick busting that hitch-post in front of Spalding.

I set my hand right up on Coly Jo's head. I think that if I set my hand up there like that it will keep that juvy ghost away. That head feels sad, like Coly Jo is crying inside, like he's on that bloodstream boat and he's hanging over the edge and mad crying like he used to cry into the back of his elbow after blackout.

"Don't cry, Coly Jo," I whisper. "Come on, man."

His hand is over my hand now. I watch his face, how the moonlight moves over it. That moonlight will do some freaky things to a face when a kid is sleeping.

I stay with Coly Jo like that for a while. I just stay next to him and pet that head of his and keep the juvy ghost away.

That blue dream light is funny. It's the color of a stove flame and it spreads wide. The smoothest part of dreaming is when you're in a plane or on a boat or riding in a train and you look over your shoulder and one of those Choate Street Honeys is in the seat next to you and she's maybe petting through that long hair of hers with one of those Mason Pearson brushes. And then she throws some eyes at you and that blue dream light floods up behind her and makes that hair look so good you think you can smell it.

You can get to smelling stuff like that in your dreams. You can smell an orange sometimes. And you can smell gasoline, too.

I was dreaming that I was on this horse with that Honey from the picture frame on Dean Petty's desk. She was sitting behind me and she had her arms around my waist and I could feel the wings of that gold butterfly pin pressing into my back, but it didn't hurt; it felt smooth. Everything was blue: the air and the birds and the ground. Even the horse breath was mad blue.

We rode out to this field and I told her I had mad love for her and she told me that she had mad love for me too and I think we were about to make some business right there on the horse. Everything was *mad* blue. That was about the smoothest dream I ever had.

I am awake now and the light has changed.

I rub my eyes and make sure the light stays the way it is. It is quieter than you can ever remember. It might be the quietest night you ever heard. No dripping faucet. No juvies snoring or choking off. You can only hear your own lungwind.

It is Long Neck's turn to sleep. I reach down and swipe at him with my pillow so he knows I'm up. I usually hit him in the head with it, but this time when I swipe, that pillow don't hit nothing but air.

I drop my head down and look, but the only thing in his bed is his pillow and Coly Jo's unbreakable comb.

That unbreakable comb looks like the loneliest unbreakable comb you'll ever see.

You can get to looking at something like that sometimes and it will start to look worse and worse. Pennies are like that. I looked at a penny once for about ten minutes. It was one of the most depressing things you could do. You just stare and stare and hear that clock ticking somewhere, and by that tenth minute you'll start to feel about as lonesome as you ever will in your life.

Maybe it's cause pennies ain't worth shit; or maybe it's cause they're all dirty and nasty-looking. At least dimes and nickels and quarters are silver and shine kind of smooth like they might be worth something. A penny just looks like an old rusty nail that got squashed. Like a nonthing. That's how that unbreakable comb looks.

When I look up at the patch window that treehand looks funny. I turn on my stomach and the moonlight is all over the window. And it's snowing those big white flakes. It's the first snow of the year and mad early for that kind of weather. But the weather will do that to you sometimes.

Something's in the treehand and it ain't a dog and it ain't a bird and it ain't a kite either. At first I think I am still dreaming, but that moonlight is white and it ain't blue at all.

Coly Jo is sitting in the dead tree. He is sporting my windbreaker and he is sitting in that dead tree like he is *part* of it, like when the tree grew he grew right along with it. And those snowflakes are falling all around him and they're all stuck in his eyelashes.

He is watching me. And he's watching me like he's been watching me for a long time, too, with his night eyes all wide and black in the middle and that scratchy half-baldy shining some in the moonlight. It's like the night cribbed Coly Jo out of his isolation room while he was sleeping, like it slipped its long dark hand through the window and put him up in those branches.

My lungwind is mad smooth now, so smooth it's like I ain't even breathing.

We watch each other for a long time like that. We watch each other the way strangers watch each other when they are walking in an alley with some bones in their pockets.

There is a part of the night that floats in your blood. It's like something from a river or a pond, and when the moon is thick it'll cook that part of the blood and make you do stuff.

The moon got my night blood up like that once when Mazzy was out dancing. I walked up to the window in the YMCA room and I dropped my drawers and let the air blow on me cool and smooth. That air felt so good I busted a sex pole.

Another time I woke up in the middle of the night and walked down to the lobby in my pajamas and fell asleep. I woke up next to the vending machine with my face all pressed against the change slot. Mazzy pulled me up by my arms and walked me back up to our room. Mazzy can do some smooth stuff like that sometimes. Sometimes she'll clean your face with some mouth spit, too.

I watch Coly Jo and he watches me. And that snow just keeps falling through the dark. It's kind of freaky cause we ain't trying to say nothing to each other. We ain't trying to make words with our mouths. We ain't using our hands. Coly Jo's got that non-look on his face and I am on my stomach. We just stay still like that and talk to each other with our eyes.

That treehand is as still as you'll ever see it. And with that snow falling it looks mad freaky. Usually some wind gets to pulling at it. It's the most silent treehand you'll ever see, I swear.

It's the kind of silence that pulls you down, down, down, to a place way behind the eyes, where the snow and the night and lungwind all blend together. It's the kind of silence that freezes you, no matter how bad you want to bust out of your patch and climb that tree. You just get frozen by that blue non-sound.

You can't even *explain* that kind of silence. You just can't.

AFTER THE AURORA HORN BLOWS, MISTER Rose comes through beating on his junk can yelling, "Flood coats! We got snow last night! Flood coats! Get em on!" So we all go back through our patch holes and throw on our flood coats.

I look for that treehand out the patch window but there's so much frost on it you can't see nothing but that white snowfreeze.

The patch feels bigger, like someone pushed the walls further apart. It's funny how two juvy bodies in a room will make that room feel smaller. I look over at my desk and see how my books are all scattered.

Long Neck ain't in the patch.

When we get outside that snow is so white it makes Hamstock look like a cake. Even that fence is white.

Your flood coat is warm and thick and when it's cold out they'll let you put your hands in the pockets. The pockets are about the smoothest part of your flood coat cause they got that thick lining in them that will cook up your hands with the quickness.

On our way to gut drill all of the juvies stop and the hoods of our flood coats flip up like a bunch of birds. Mister Rose is busting it toward the dead tree. He is busting it like you've never seen him bust it before.

I look up in that tree and my Red Troutman's fireproof windbreaker is hanging still from those high branches. And next to my windbreaker are Coly Jo's jeans and his only pair of drawers. Then I look down at the base of the tree and Mister Rose has stopped and dropped to his knees and he is pounding on the ground.

There is a big dark splot in the snow. Coly Jo's body is all heaped up there. Coly Jo's body is naked and frosted with snow and that half-baldy's got a crack in it. And the way his eyes are bugging out and the way his arm is twisted all backwards around his neck you just know he won't be getting up.

Coly Jo's body has turned into a non-body. It's the kind of non-body that you can't even stick a name on. It's the kind of non-body that you might see on one of Deacon Bob Fly's splot cards.

Now Mister Rose is howling out and pounding on Coly Jo's chest like he's trying to get that breath smoking from his mouth. You would think that a juvy body would make that snow melt around it. You would think that the blood would still cook up enough to let that last breath smoke out. You would think that even a naked non-body might leak *something* out of the mouth.

Mister Rose stops pounding on Coly Jo and then he takes his flood coat off. Those shark eyes are glazed. He lays that flood coat over Coly Jo and tells us to go inside.

All the other juvies turn around and go back into Spalding. But I walk over to the dead tree and look up in those branches.

You would think some wind would blow that stuff free. You would think that Whoever makes a kid wind up all heaped up at the bottom of a dead tree like that might be smooth enough to blow his stuff out of those branches when it's all over.

You can't just leave stuff in a dead tree like that; you just can't.

Back in my patch I can't move so smooth and it feels like the joints in my arms and my legs are locking up on me. It feels like I am walking through something thick. It's hard to walk when your patch is thick like that. It's hard to get those legs moving when your joints are all locked up.

I walk over to my desk and look at how my books got scattered. Then I start to stack them. When you stack stuff like that it helps you lose some of that thick feeling. You can stack most things: plates or boxes or magazines. Mazzy likes to do that sometimes when something's heavy on her head. She'll start stacking some magazines for a while, and if those thoughts are still heavy, she'll just scatter those magazines and start stacking them again.

In that memory I get she always starts stacking stuff. After the skinny guy with the beard hits her in the face with the phonebook and leaves, she always sits down next to the sink with a bunch of dirty plates in her arms and starts to stack them real slow.

But I don't got none of that stuff, so I just start stacking my books like I'm getting ready for slate docket.

Outside you can hear that ambulance horn and you can hear those men talking into their radios and you can see lights flashing, but you don't want to look cause you are too busy stacking those books. *Just stack those books now,* you tell yourself. *Get ready for slate docket.*

When I am finished stacking them I pull out my history book and open it. Then I start flipping through the pages. And I turn that book upside down and shake it about twelve times. But the only thing that falls out of it is that letter from Mazzy.

Somebody turns that siren off but those lights keep flashing outside.

I look back at my history book. That Hurricane map is gone.

Long gone.

DEAN PETTY IS SITTING BEHIND HIS BIG iron desk. There's this man I ain't never seen before sitting next to him. He's holding a metal clipboard. The man with the clipboard takes some gum out of his pocket and offers me a stick. I don't take it. Then he offers me a mint from his other pocket and I don't take that either.

After he grubs on his gum for a minute he takes his glasses off and cleans them with part of his shirt and puts them back on. All you can hear are those parts in that clock that's ticking.

"You know why you've been called down here, Mister Sura?" the man asks.

"No sir," I say.

"Can I call you Sura?" he asks.

"Yes sir," I say. It's funny how Dean Petty won't even look at you, like he's just a cold glass of water or something. Dean Smoothy.

"Did Mister Sheridan make any indication at all as to what his plans were?" the man asks.

"Who's Mister Sheridan?" I ask.

"Did he tell you where he was planning to go?" the man asks.

"I don't know no Mister Sheridan," I say.

"Did your *patch mate* give you any clues as to what his plans were, Sura?" the man asks.

"Long Neck?" I say.

"You can help yourself by helping us, Sura," the man says. "If you know anything that can help us catch him we'd appreciate it. You'd appreciate it, too."

The man with the clipboard looks over at Dean Petty. Dean Petty looks back at him. They talk to each other with their eyes.

I hate how Dean Petty still won't even look at you. I hate how he's got his feet all propped up on the desk like he's on the beach and he's about to order some frozen drinks or something.

I look on his desk at that Honey in the picture frame. If she's his kid I can't imagine what he does to her. He probably busts her in the ass with that paddle if she don't get her homework right or something. He probably takes that paddle home in his briefcase and hangs it on a hook over the TV. She probably has to creep around the house like a cat just so she won't get swatted. I can't imagine that Honey being his kid.

"You can shorten your clip a little, Sura," the man with the clipboard says with all of those smooth sounds in his voice. "According to our records, your clip still has some weight to it. We'd be willing to lighten it a bit."

This guy with the clipboard wouldn't know me from a can of grease and he's trying to talk to me like that. Offering me shit from his pockets. Throwing those looks at Dean Petty. Grubbing the flavor out of that gum.

"I don't know nothin," I say.

"You don't know nothin," he says. He tries to say it the same way I said it, too.

"We didn't talk much," I say. Then he throws another look over at Dean Petty and Dean Petty nods his head and makes his hands into a triangle on his desk. You just *know* that Dean Petty is making that triangle with his hands cause he saw some guy in a *movie* doing it. You have to wonder about guys who do stuff like that. You just *know* that Dean Petty does stuff like that all the time. He probably goes around clicking his heels together and shit like that. Good old Dean Smoothy.

"If he left you any hints or suggestions . . ." the man with the clipboard says, but I just let that voice of his fade out like some TV snow.

I'm too busy looking at that picture of the Honey on Dean Petty's desk. I start to see her in the same way she was in my dream. I see her hair and her eyes and her mouth and that blue light glowing smooth behind her. And we are on that horse and those horse feet are clopping like some heartbeats and I can feel her hand around my waist and some tree branches are hanging down in front of us and I am pushing those branches out of her way with the back of my hands and I can still feel that gold butterfly pin pressing into my back and it feels nice and we're whispering mad love to each other and we are laughing like we got our chocolate milk bellies up and that blue light is as blue as some light can get . . .

Something's got me by the wrist. My wristbone feels like it's going to pop. When I look up Dean Petty is mad squeezing it.

"Let go of it, son," the man with the clipboard keeps saying. "Let go of it."

Dean Petty's face is mad red now. It looks like it's going to bust. He's got those fire-hands, too, and they're making that picture frame vibrate like it's electric.

After I let go his hands are still shaking. That blue light is white now. Everything in the room seems cleaner for some reason. It takes a minute for that blood to leave Dean Petty's face. After he smooths out his lungwind he sticks that picture in a drawer and closes the drawer, and he closes it like he ain't never going to open it again.

Then he asks the man with the clipboard to leave his office for a minute and the man says, "Sure," and adjusts his clipboard and steps off out into the hallway. Then Dean Petty lets the blinds down and sets me up over his big iron desk and spreads my feet and slides my drawers down and reaches for that paddle and swats that chocolate milk belly right out of me.

He don't even bother to write nothing on the blackboard this time.

After the sixth one I stop counting. *You ain't crying,* I tell myself. *Don't do it, Sura.* You can always bust a good cry back in your patch. I just keep swallowing those swats.

That's okay, though, I think. Maybe he'll break the paddle on my ass so he won't be able to take it home and hang it over his TV.

With every *Wop!* I just close my eyes and think about that blue light . . .

You don't walk too smooth after some Dean Smoothy swats. You get the wobbles like you ain't never had them in your life, I swear. You get those fire-hands, too. The worst part about it is when a juvy is waiting for you at the rabbit line and you got your hands all pressed up against your back and you're trying to rub the feeling back into your ass and he says, "I'll race you, Sura, I'll race you." And then you look and at the other end of the rabbit line you can see about ten juvies and they're flipping their juvy pounds around and betting on the race.

You try to tell yourself that you can do it, that you can make your mind clean the pain out. You try to tell yourself that the stinging will go away once the blood is cooked up for a race, that once that wind is in your hair everything will go light and smooth and those knees will be pumping. You try to tell yourself all of that stuff, but then you take your hands out of your drawers and you see some blood. And you hold it up and turn your hand so you can see how red it is, and that juvy who wants to race you sees it, too, and he gets that haunted-house look up on his face and then he's off with the quickness and he's shouting and screaming like some boogymonsters are chasing him.

Nurse Rushing is cleaning my ass with some stuff that smells like paint.

"Looks like he got you pretty good," she says.

"Yes, ma'am," I say.

"Too good," she says.

That stuff that smells like paint mad stings, but not like it did that first time I got swatted; that was like some bees. This time it's like there's a funny bone in my ass, like that feeling you get when you turn a radio up loud and press it up against you.

"Can you sit?" Nurse Rushing asks.

"No, ma'am," I say.

"He really got you," she says.

"Is it broke?" I ask. I heard about how this kid around my way fell off a mini-bike and broke his assbone and had to lay up on his stomach for two months.

"It's not broken," Nurse Rushing says.

"Feels like it is," I say.

"I'm sure it does," she says.

I look on her desk and see a file folder with Coly Jo's name on it. Nurse Rushing can see how I'm looking at it and she looks at me all funny and then she looks away. She's rubbing some medicine cream on me now.

"Are they gonna bury him?" I ask.

"Excuse me?"

"Coly Jo," I say. "Are they gonna put him in a body-box and bury him?"

Nurse Rushing don't answer. She's too busy rubbing in that medicine. Then she looks back at that file folder with Coly Jo's name on it and goes, "I imagine they will, Sura."

You can't just *imagine* something like that. Putting a kid in a body-box and putting that body-box in the ground is something you got to know about. If you don't put a non-body in a body-box and stick that body-box in the ground or burn it with some fire, that non-body will never get no sleep, and then you got another juvy ghost walking around and howling and shit.

Nurse Rushing finishes with that medicine cream. Then she takes off those rubber gloves and wipes those smooth hands on a hospital rag and takes that file and looks at it for a minute and sticks it in a drawer.

"Poor kid," Nurse Rushing says.

I hate how she says that; like she says it to the *file*; like Coly Jo ain't a juvy or a kid no more; like he's just a bunch of papers in a *file*. I would hate it if someone said *Poor Sura* like that. The last thing in the world you want is to hear someone say that. I ain't kidding.

THEY DON'T GIVE ME A NEW PATCH MATE. Sleeping alone is kind of freaky. The only lungwind you hear is yours and the only bunk noises you hear are yours and the only thoughts in your patch besides your patch's thoughts are your own.

And everything else—that faucet dripping and that wind whistling through the frost on your window and that hall breath—all of it—sounds about four times louder, like that other juvy who used to sleep below you soaked up some of those noise waves.

You even think you can hear those little touchdown songs in your electronic football game, and you ain't heard that in weeks.

And every time Mister Rose makes that final Spalding sweep you just hate him more. You hate him cause he just walks around like nothing happened, like that snow outside covered up Coly Jo's body splot and everything is back to counting clicks and carping and beating on junk cans and shit. You hate him cause you want to look at his face and see that there's part of it that might be different, like those nasty shark eyes might be softer, or he might be wearing his Afro lower, or maybe he's got a new space between his teeth or something like that. But when you look at him you just get that fist up in your stomach cause ain't nothing changed. And now that fist's got some glass with it, too.

After blackout you spend a lot of time checking that bottom bunk; like when you look, Coly Jo or Long Neck or someone is just going to be laying up there. And he'll start to cry into the back of his elbow or bump at the gums about getting the Flaptooth or pick mouth scabs or point some finger guns at you or something.

And you spend a lot of time trying to *not*-look out your window at the treehand, even though that frost is still there. Every time you catch your neck turning toward that patch window you just say *Stop, neck* or you pinch yourself on the side so that you won't look. Cause if you look out at that treehand you just know something is going to be in it.

That might be the hardest part about sleeping alone—trying to not-look at that treehand. It's hard to not-look, though, especially when your windbreaker is still hanging from it. Especially when it's been up there for mad days like that and nobody's even bothered to take it down. It's like it's *tied* there or something. Like it's grown into the tree; like it's a *flag* or something.

When you sleep you try to not-dream. You just try to float around in that bloodstream boat. But you don't want to float too far away in case a night creeper slips in through your patch hole.

You try to keep one eye open. You can close one eye

but that other one is steady on that patch hole light. And your ears get to opening up more so that they can hear those juvy feet shuffling and those whisper-voices. You start to train yourself to have some Indian ears.

You've heard how fish can breathe with their eyes and shit like that. Opening those ears is kind of like making them breathe.

Busting a half-sleep ain't so bad once you get the hang of it. Fish float around when they sleep.

So that clip starts to wind down and those days get shorter and that light fades faster and your breath is mad smoking whenever you're outside. The snow gets so hard that if you slip and fall it feels like getting blasted with a bow. After your assbone heals and the feeling comes back, you make yourself strong for those last few weeks.

You learn how to get through each day so it goes by fast. You learn how to make the parts of your body harder and tighter. You make a fist and hold that fist as long as you can, cause it makes the bone in your arm stronger. You got to make your bones stronger than the weather. You got to make your stomach thicker and you got to learn how to make your blood cook hotter, cause you got to fight that wind that whistles through the frost in your patch window.

You stop busting pisses at the Telescope Pit and when a juvy comes up to you with those happy feet and he wants to run the rabbit line you just shake your head and say something about the snow.

You even stop questioning Boo at the juvy pound line. You just give him those six tenths so he won't give you no static.

Aurora horn to gut drill to shower room to first hash to slate docket to second hash to slate docket to third hash to study box to free time to blackout. It's just like that. You don't bother playing floor hockey in the basement no more and you don't bother sneaking down to the sweet spot after blackout to hear those skin flicks, either. You just play the rest of that clip out. It's like setting a fire in a junk can and waiting for that fire to die. Sometimes the can starts to burn after all of the junk inside it has turned to ash. Hamstock is like that can now.

You don't even notice it when the night guard comes back. All of the sudden you just start hearing those clicks again. But it's like those clicks are coming from something else now, like those clicks weren't from the night guard's ribstick busting that hitchpost in the first place. You start to think that those clicks were part of a big invisible clock that the night cribbed. Like the night was hanging out outside the fence with its long greedy fingers, out in those bean fields somewhere, just waiting for the chance to crib that clock. And while those clicks were gone all this bad shit happened with Coly Jo and Demetrius Gord and Long Neck, and now everything is supposed to be back to normal again.

But those bones feel different somehow. They feel like they ache; like they got something cold in them.

Deacon Bob Fly is drinking some coffee. That steam is rising up in his eyes and when it mixes with that sweat on his face it makes his face look mad greasy.

There ain't no storybooks today, and there ain't no thumb puppets and there ain't no splot cards, neither. He's just sitting at his desk drinking that coffee. That notebook is closed for once. Usually it's all open and that pen is up in his hand and he's ready to bust that chicken scratch.

I've been looking down at my shoes a lot lately. Somehow looking down at your shoes makes everything seem a little easier. What's kind of smooth about it is that you usually don't notice your shoes all that much. When you're roller skating you notice your *skates* cause they might have some of those thick neon wheels that glow in the dark, or they might have those ball bearings that get to making that smooth spinning sound, but a lot of that is for the *Honeys*, and you're *supposed* to notice that shit. But the shoes you wear every day around Hamstock just become part of everything else and you don't care so much about them. They just start to take the shape of everything else. They just become part of Hamstock.

Deacon Bob Fly finishes his coffee and wipes that grease off of his face with his hand.

"So tomorrow's the day, huh, Sura?" Deacon Bob asks.

". . . Yeah," I say. Deacon Bob looks in his coffee cup like there's something in there. Like there's a word in there that he can use to make everything seem smooth. He keeps looking into his cup for that word and then he looks up.

"You looking forward to going home?" he asks.

". . . Yeah," I say again. I've been saying *Yeah* a lot to Deacon Bob lately. It makes it easier to look at your shoes. You can just say *Yeah* and look down.

"Your mother called me today," Deacon Bob says. "She said she has your room all fixed up."

". . . Yeah," I say again.

"You must be looking forward to going back to regular school again."

I just nod my head. Deacon Bob is back to looking for that word in his coffee cup. It's funny how he's always trying to talk to me about stuff but he never really knows what to say. It would be kind of smooth if he talked to me about the Honeys or some foreign rides or shit like that. But he's too busy looking in books and busting chicken scratch and talking about that goonfish story. He's too busy doing what you're *supposed* to do.

"Is there anything you want to say, Sura?" Deacon Bob asks.

I just shake my head.

"Do you feel like you've made your reform?" he asks.

". . . Yeah," I say.

"Is there anything you would like to do before you leave?" he asks. "Anything you feel you need to *complete*?"

I think about that for a minute. I think about how I would like my Dy-no-mite shirt back the way it was so it's got those letters fixed and so it ain't all stretched out in the shoulders, and I think about how I would like to have my electronic football game back, and I think about how I would like all of those juvy pounds back from Boo

Boxfoot so I could buy a whole case of blow-pops as soon as I get out, and I think about how I would like to have that Dean Petty paddle for a couple of hours and how I would like to go around Hamstock with it and swat some people.

I think about how I would swat Dean Smoothy as many times as he swatted me and how I would swat that guy with the clipboard and how I would swat the night guard and how I would swat the Mop Man for giving those pliers to Boo Boxfoot and how I would swat Mister Rose until he bled and had to go to Nurse Rushing's office to get that paint medicine spread on his ass. But I don't say none of that.

"What is it, Sura? What would you like to do?"

"Huh?" I say. I don't really hear him cause I'm too busy untying my shoes.

"This is your chance to say what you want, Sura," Deacon Bob says. I got one of my shoes off now.

"The tree," I say.

"What tree?" Deacon Bob asks.

"The dead tree," I say. Now I got the other one off, too.

"What about it?" Deacon Bob asks.

"I'd chop that shit down," I say.

We sit there like that for a minute. Deacon Bob is scratching his yellow head and looking for that word in his coffee cup again. When I start to hear those parts in his desk clock I push my shoes under his desk and get up and turn around and walk back to Spalding in the snow.

When you dig through some snow it's kind of hard cause those fingers go numb with the quickness. And when you start digging into the ground it's even harder cause that snow has made it hard like a street.

I am sitting in front of the dead tree and I am digging in the same spot where I saw Coly Jo bury whatever it was that he wrapped in that nose rag. It's hard to find exactly where a kid buries something. If you were a dog you could just sniff it out, but juvies don't got brains in their noses.

So I dig up three different spots and my socks are mad wet and my hands are pink from the cold and there is some steam rising off of them, and I finally find that white nose rag.

It's funny how the ground will make a nose rag look all brown and nasty, like it's dead or something. I stick my hand into the ground and pull that folded cloth out. It's mad stiff, but I pull at those folds so it opens up.

It's kind of smooth how the tail of that squirrel-skin cap just falls out and hits the snow. You'd think the ground would have grubbed it up and turned it into some bugs. You'd think that squirrel tail would have a bunch of horseflies on it or something, but it don't.

It's funny how there ain't no one around when you leave Hamstock. All of those juvies are in slate docket and it makes everything look sad. It makes that fence look bigger somehow.

That depot van is waiting for you down in the parking lot. When you look out the window of Dean Petty's office you can see the old guy reading the paper behind the windshield, and you can see that security meshing that divides the front of the van from the back.

I am wearing these slippers that Mazzy sent to me after my first week here. This is the first time I'm wearing them. I also got a letter that came for me today. Other than that, it's just me and that squirrel tail in my pocket.

Dean Petty is sitting at his iron desk and he's got those release papers in front of him and he's signing them and pulling the different colored papers off and sticking them in a file with my name on it. That picture of that Honey is back on the desk.

Dean Petty turns around for his stapler and staples some stuff and then faces me again. Then he stamps some stuff on those papers and turns around again and sticks some of them in a different file.

When he is finished he looks up and points at me to take a seat. I sit down and we look at each other for a few minutes. He makes that triangle with his hands again. I just want to get those papers and get on that van and close the door and sit behind that security mesh and watch Hamstock shrink into those bean fields like something in the fog.

"They found him, you know," Dean Petty says. It's the first time he's ever said shit to me. His voice is exactly like you'd think it would be, all hard and even, like that throatbox is made out of some rusty metal.

"Long Neck?" I say.

"He went back home to his father's house," Dean Petty says. I don't say nothing. I just sit there.

"He tried to shoot him with a homemade gun," Dean Petty says.

I don't say nothing to that neither.

"Blew up in his hand," Dean Petty says. Then he fixes a pile of papers on his desk and brushes his fingers over it. "He lost it."

"What?" I ask.

"His hand," Dean Petty says. "He lost it."

"Damn," I say.

"They sent him down to Cairo."

"What's that?" I ask.

"Southern tip of the state," Dean Petty says. "Maximum security." Then he signs two more pieces of paper and gives one to me and sticks the other one in my file and looks at me with those blank eyes like he wants me to leave.

"Dean Petty, can I ask you something?" I say.

"That van out there is gonna leave you," he says. "You got about five seconds."

"You ever go roller skating?" I ask. Dean Petty's face changes. For a second you think he might be seeing himself at the roller rink with some wristbands on his arms and a smooth windbreaker and a Honey on his hip. And maybe that Casablanca light is spinning around and moving over his face like a good Casablanca light will do. But then you see those eyes shift back to what they were and you think he's going to take those papers back out of your file and tear them up and carp you and send you back to Spalding. But he don't do that, neither. He just stares at that triangle he made with his hands. Then he looks up and shakes his head and points me out the door.

I turn around with my release papers and walk out. It will be pretty smooth driving in that depot van with that picture of his daughter to look at. You can look at a picture and in your mind you can turn that picture into a movie.

You can call the movie *Roller-Skate Love,* starring Dean Smoothy's daughter and good old Sura. And all the scenes can happen at the roller rink. In your mind you can watch that movie over and over and over . . .

WHEN YOU GET OUT, YOU FEEL FUNNY. Your body is used to walking that path to the hash house and that path to slate docket and that path to juvy pound line and that path to Nurse Rushing's office and all of those paths. Your body just wants to move in one direction.

When you get out, there *ain't no* slate docket and there *ain't no* hash house and there *ain't no* Spalding Cottage. Instead there are stores and houses and rides and little kids falling down in the snow and stuff like that.

You start to feel like the parts of your body can move in new directions, like something's changed in the way your bones are put together.

You might see something shiny on the street and you think it's a quarter and you can just walk right over to it and pick it up and stick it in your pocket. You can do that and no one is going to go *Lock up, Sura!* and no one is going to carp you or stick you in pushup position or swat you or nothing. You can just pick that quarter up and stick it in your pocket.

But what's funny is that right after you do it, you get

that old feeling back up in your bones—just for a second; that same feeling you get when it's after blackout and Mister Rose is making that final sweep. You get that feeling that the night's got something up its sleeve for you. Even if it's during the *day* you get that feeling.

So that van drops me off at Flintlock's house, and that tetherball pole *is* fixed and that plastic bag *is* off the window and there's a *new* window. I walk to the side of the house and look in through the window.

Flintlock and Mazzy are laying up on a couch and the room is dark and all you can see is that blue light from the TV glowing soft on their faces. Mazzy's got her fishing hat on with the front flipped up. They look mad comfortable. Flintlock's got some long hippie hair and his face looks a lot older than Mazzy's. But they look happy. You feel like you want to knock on the door but you don't. For some reason you don't feel like you can go inside yet.

No one found my hoody bag. I hid it in a coffee can and stuck it under this old drain pipe. When I open it, those hoodies make that *clink, clink* sound and my knot of bones feels nice and thick in my hand. I sling my hoody bag over my shoulder and walk away from the reservoir. It's all frozen over like some thermometer juice.

You can't put a hoody back on, but you can tape it to the car you cribbed it from. I am in Good Oaks now and I got some electricity tape and I take that '75 Benzo 280 hoody and tape it to the front of that smooth ride. It don't matter that there's a new one on there. You just want to put it back.

After I tape that hoody back on, I go over to this other neighborhood and tape two more hoodies back on. This Oldsmobile didn't even bother to get a new one.

When I am finished with the hoodies I think about Slider and how I wrote him about breaking north with my knot of bones, and I think about jumping on that freight train that goes over the train bridge and how I could just sit on top of some coal or something. But those thoughts just fade away like some garbage blowing on the street.

I picture what it's going to be like when Slider gets out of St. Chuck's, about what kind of shit we'll get into, but after a minute I can't see myself in the picture. It's like someone took an eraser and cleaned the image of myself out of my mind. And then I don't see nothing, just some dirty snow that a dog shitted on.

I step over it and walk back to Flintlock's house.

When you knock on a screen door it gets kind of loud. And when you hear those feet shuffling toward you on some carpeting and you hear that familiar voice saying stuff, you start to get that chocolate milk belly up with the quickness.

And when that door opens and you see your moms with that fishing hat on and the bill flipped up, that's about the best thing you could see. We hug each other and she cleans something off of my face and then she calls me by my first name. Man, it's smooth to hear your moms call you by your first name like that. I go, "Hey, Moms," and we hug each other harder.

When that screen door closes I take my coat off and hang it in this little closet by the door. Something smells mad good. That's about the best smell there is—food that's cooking in a kitchen. If you ever want to get in a good mood, start cooking something in your kitchen and then go for a walk outside and come back in an hour. When you open that door, that warm, spicy smell is mad thick and takes the fist right out of your stomach.

Something in those Sura bones feels like home.

In my room I walk up to my window and look out at the train bridge. That little piece of stained glass is smooth. The snow makes everything look good and sanitized. When you look through that piece of stained glass it makes everything look purple.

I take that letter out of my pocket and open it up. It's that Hurricane map. No note or nothing; just the map. Long Neck just sent it by itself. I look through that stained glass again and the sky is starting to fall out. Then I look back down at the Hurricane map and I see that his map sky is almost the same purple color.

When you look even closer at that map sky you see some mad bugged-out shit. It's the first time you've ever seen it, too. You must have studied that map a hundred times, but you never looked at Hurricane's map sky like that.

Way up in the corner of that sky Hurricane drew this little floppy "V," and the way it is drawn it looks like a bird. That little bird up there is so smooth I almost get that chocolate milk belly up again. I am smiling like you smile when you got a Choate Street Honey on your hip at the roller rink and she's tugging on those wristbands.

I stare at that little bird for almost an entire click, and toward the end of that click, when the real sky in my window starts making those darker violet colors, I start thinking that *Coly Jo* is that little V-bird way up there in that Hurricane sky. And he's got that shag he always wanted. And he's sporting a kung fu housecoat with some powers in it. And he's got that kung fu *dog,* too. And his chocolate milk belly is up and he's laughing and those gums of his are shining just like his baldy used to. That's the fattest bird, you'll ever see, too, Sura, I tell myself. But that bird is mad flying.

And just like that I am crying like a little kid. And I am swallowing that sound hard, like you swallow a sandwich that's too thick.

Then I take that picture of Dean Petty's daughter and put it on this bedside stand that Flintlock made for me. I say good night to her and close my eyes and wait for that bloodstream boat to take me to that blue light.

For some reason a picture of that new cinder track at the junior high appears in my head. I am on that track all by myself. I am on that track and I am running as fast as I can, but it ain't like I'm trying to run fast to beat nobody. Those cinders are kicking up behind me and I am just running.

ADAM RAPP, already an award-winning novelist, playwright, and director, is now an acclaimed filmmaker, too. His plays include *Nocturne, Ghosts in the Cottonwoods, Animals and Plants, Blackbird, Stone Cold Dead Serious, Finer Noble Gases, Faster, Trueblinka, Dreams of the Salthorse, Gompers,* and *Red Light Winter.* His new play, *Essential Self-Defense,* will open in 2007. The author's other works include the young adult novels *Missing the Piano, The Copper Elephant, Little Chicago, 33 Snowfish,* and *Under the Wolf, Under the Dog,* the graphic novel *Decelerate Blue,* and the adult novel *The Year of Endless Sorrows.* Mr. Rapp's first feature film, *Winter Passing,* starring Ed Harris, Will Ferrell, and Zooey Deschanel, had its world premiere as an Official Selection of the Toronto International Film Festival and was released in February 2006. He is currently finishing his second feature film, *Blackbird,* which he adapted from his play. Mr. Rapp is a graduate of Clarke College in Dubuque, Iowa, and completed a two-year playwriting fellowship at Juilliard. He was born in Chicago, Illinois, and makes his home in New York City.